Dreaded dreamscape

"But..." said Paul, completely bewildered, "but how do *you* know about it?"

"Because I'm having it too." She sank down into the desk across from him. "Every night. A terrible dream. The field, and the glowing thing, and I can hardly move, and that horrible feeling that something's about to happen, that I have to do something. And there's a person standing next to me. And last night I saw that it was you.... I could hardly believe it...and I *had* to find out!"

"You mean," Paul blurted out, "you mean you are trying to tell me that you—*you*, Francine—are having *my* dream?"

into the
dream

WILLIAM

SLEATOR

illustrated by ruth sanderson

BULLSEYE BOOKS

ALFRED A. KNOPF • NEW YORK

A BULLSEYE BOOK PUBLISHED BY ALFRED A. KNOPF, INC.
Copyright © 1979 by William Sleator
Illustrations copyright © 1979 by Ruth Sanderson
Cover art © 1991 by Doron Ben-Ami

Library of Congress Catalog Card Number: 78-11825
ISBN: 0-679-80348-3
RL: 5.7
First Bullseye Books edition: August 1991

Manufactured in the United States of America
10 9 8 7 6 5 4 3 2 1

This book is dedicated to Helen Londe,
the real Cookie, who is not a Newfoundland,
but who did give immeasurable help
to Paul, Francine, and Noah—
not to mention the author.

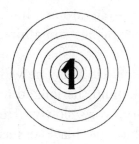

The first dream did not seem strange to him. It was night; he was standing at the edge of a large empty field, trying to move toward a glowing object floating over the center of the field.

It was a particularly vivid dream. He had such a strong sense of really being there, that when he awoke in the middle of the night, he did not know for a moment where he was. But then dreams are often vivid, and Paul did not remember it—until several nights later, when the dream came again.

This time there were several differences. He seemed a little closer to the glowing object, though he still could not tell what it was. To the left he could see an unfamiliar low building with the word *Stardust* floating over it. But the most striking difference was a relentless feeling of urgency that pulsed in the air around him. Something terrible was about to happen—something that only he could prevent.

His whole body was tense with fear. He knew he was being watched. He longed to look behind, he longed to run. But he could only move very, very slowly. He inched his way painfully through the thick blackness as the terror all around him rose to a screaming pitch.

And then suddenly there was a small figure in white dashing toward the light, pursued by a dark hulking creature that he could not identify. Paul awoke to the sound of his own cry in the dark bedroom, the terror still with him.

At school the next day he could not get the dream out of his mind. Miss Keck was amazed and disappointed when he misspelled *shenanigans*. And then, to make it worse, Francine Gill, one of the silliest girls in the class, spelled it right.

Paul was rather shamefaced when he joined Larry, his best friend, at recess. He tried to explain away his stupid mistake by telling Larry about the dream. But Larry did not seem to understand.

"It doesn't seem so strange to me," he said. "People always have repeating dreams."

"Yes, but . . . it's so hard to explain," said Paul. "There was a *feeling*, as though something really horrible was about to happen, and I had to do something to

2

STARDUST

stop it, right away. It was so scary and realistic, I never had a dream that was so—"

Larry grabbed his arm. "Hey, let's get out of here! Mr. Rogers is going to try to rope us into that stupid basketball game. Come on!"

Then Paul began having the dream every night, and every night it grew more intense. He began to be aware of voices. They were all around him, incoherently babbling, mumbling, and whispering words that he could not understand. When he awoke he would be mumbling the sounds urgently to himself, trying to make them out.

One day his mother asked him why he had been talking in his sleep. He insisted that he didn't remember doing it. His mother was a scientist, and he did not want to tell her about the dream. Though the dream was frightening, it was also becoming very important to him in some odd way, and he did not want to see her laugh it off as something "psychological," as he knew she would. After that, he closed the door of his room firmly when he went to bed at night.

Though the dream was, indeed, becoming an increasingly important experience, something to be guarded and protected, he did make one more stab at talking to Larry about it. He and Larry were the best students in the class, and had always understood one another. But the dream, it seemed, was coming between them now. Larry took off his glasses and looked up at Paul with a speculative expression.

4

"Maybe you're going schizo," he said thoughtfully. "I read a story about that once. There was a kid who kept thinking about snow all the time. It was the only thing he ever thought about. And he stopped caring about anything else, and all he ever wanted to do was—"

"No, it's not like that at all," Paul said, and walked away.

He was so angry that he did not look where he was going, and suddenly he found himself stumbling right into the middle of the group of silly girls that he and Larry were always trying to ignore. The girls put their hands over their mouths and giggled at him, and one of them, Francine Gill, said, "What's the hurry, Paul? Recess just started. Are you running back to the room to do some extra studying?"

Paul glared. Francine was the one who had spelled *shenanigans* right when he had missed it, and he still resented her for it. "No," he said. "I just . . . oh, skip it."

Their laughter rose up behind him as he hurried away.

Every night the dream was sharper and more real. The feeling of danger grew, weighed down upon him, until he felt like screaming as he struggled there, moving so slowly, just a little closer each night. *Stardust* blinking to his left, the voices murmuring around him, the little figure in white dashing toward the glowing object, the great hulking creature close behind—what was about to happen? Would he reach the light in time? And would there be safety there, or more danger, or some daring and difficult act to perform?

Behind the murmuring voices, he began to be aware of another sound, a strange, almost mechanical whining that rose and fell, unearthly and penetrating. And what were the voices saying? One word did seem to be repeated more often than the others, "*Jaleela, jaleeeeela, jaleeeeeela!*" What were they trying to tell him?

And then one night he noticed that someone was standing beside him in the dream. It was something of a shock, because until that moment he had been aware of no one but himself watching the terrifying scene. This person too seemed to be struggling toward the glowing sphere with as much difficulty as he was having. And each night after that, the person was a little clearer, but still too indistinct for him to see who it was. At first he resented the person's presence, but as time went on he began to feel a longing to make contact, to reach out to whoever it was. Somehow that was vital; it was the only hope for safety.

The whining was closer now, rising and falling, accompanied by a high keening wind. The glowing object was brighter, beckoning them to follow it, urging them on. But they had to move so slowly! The terrible urgency and fear rang like panic through his body.

Hostile creatures were watching them, invisible, but about to burst upon them. And then the figure in white, dancing toward the light, almost upon it now. And the hulking thing close behind. And suddenly the awful feeling of lurching into space, and blackness.

Paul did not talk to Larry anymore, or to anyone else for that matter. He took to spending recess and lunchtime alone in the empty classroom, thinking about the dream. Though Miss Keck sometimes shot him a worried glance as she left, no one came to bother him, and he grew to treasure this private time. It was therefore annoyance he felt, as much as surprise, when one day he heard a footstep and looked up to see that girl Francine again, standing in the doorway.

She had never shown any interest in him before, regarding him, he was sure, with the same contempt that he felt for her. But now she was staring at him intensely.

She pushed a wisp of blonde hair out of her eyes. "Paul," she said in an unusually hesitant voice. "Paul, I . . . Last night the light got brighter, and . . . Oh, it *is* you standing next to me on the field, I *know* it's you!"

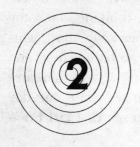

She took a step toward him. "Paul, say something!" she said sharply. "*Is* it you standing there? Next to me, on the field?"

Any connection between this girl and the dream seemed so utterly improbable to Paul that it was almost as if the words had not come from Francine but from somewhere else. And so he could think of nothing to say.

"Well? Is it you?" repeated Francine.

"But . . ." said Paul, completely bewildered, "but how do *you* know about it?"

"Because I'm having it too." She sank down into the desk across from him. "Every night. A terrible dream.

The field, and the glowing thing, and I can hardly move, and that horrible feeling that something's about to happen, that I have to do something. And there's a person standing next to me. And last night I saw that it was you. . . . I could hardly believe it . . . and I *had* to find out!"

"You mean," he blurted out, "you mean you are trying to tell me that you— *you*, Francine—are having *my* dream?"

"What do you think I've been *saying* for the last ten minutes? I thought you were supposed to be such a brain." She turned away from him.

"But . . . but, I—"

"And it *would* be you, of all people," she said bitterly, expressing his own feeling exactly. "A stuck-up boy who never does anything but *read*. I'll just have to rescue that kid all by myself."

"Rescue what kid?"

She pursed her lips and shook her head angrily. "I wish I hadn't said anything to you. Don't you remember a thing?"

"But Francine!" He stepped toward her and gripped her arm. "What—"

There was a commotion in the doorway, and the other students burst noisily into the room. Paul and Francine did their best to scramble hastily apart, but it was still obvious to everyone that something had been happening between them—a situation acutely embarrassing to them both. Without a glance in his direction, Francine bustled over to her friends, and Paul slunk off to his seat, turning away from all the others. Fortunately, Miss Keck returned at that moment and restored order before any real wisecracking could start.

Now Paul could think about nothing but getting to Francine after school and finding out what she had been talking about. The rest of the day was torture. But when at last school did let out, Miss Keck called Paul up to her desk.

"Paul, I've been meaning to talk to you for quite a while," she said, as everyone else, including Francine, left the room.

Paul just stood there, twisting his hands and shuffling his feet, longing desperately to leave and find Francine before she left the school yard, for he had no idea where she lived. "I . . . I'm sort of in a hurry, Miss Keck," he said. "Could we talk . . . another time? Tomorrow? Right now I—"

"Paul, I know something's on your mind. You've been so distracted. You never pay attention in class anymore, and you're really falling behind in your work." She leaned toward him with a concerned expression. "If you're having some problem, at home, or with your friends, I wish you would tell me about it. You were one of the best students in the class, and now, frankly, I'm worried about you."

"Oh, no, Miss Keck, there's nothing wrong. Really." He craned his neck briefly toward the window, trying to catch a glimpse of Francine. Then he turned back. "I . . . just . . . I've been doing a lot of reading on my own, I guess, and not enough homework. But I'll get back to it, I promise. But right now I really have to get—"

She shook her head. "I'm really disappointed in you. This isn't like the Paul Rhodes I used to know. I'm trying to be fair, and talk to you about it first. But now I'm afraid I'm going to have to let your mother know how your work has been falling off."

"Oh, no, Miss Keck, *please*. I . . . I *will* talk to you another time, I just can't today. And I promise you my work will get better. Could you please wait? Just a little while?"

Now there was annoyance in her voice. "Oh, all right, Paul, I'll give you one more chance. But if I don't see a change in you right away, I'm going to have to talk to your mother. For your own good." She shuffled some papers while he waited tensely. "You may go now," she said at last, and he dashed out of the room.

The school yard was nearly empty, and Francine was nowhere in sight. He ran frantically from one end of the blacktop to the other, then around to the back of the school. There, just when he was about to give up hope, he saw a group of girls standing outside the fence, and a blonde head among them.

He was panting when he reached them, and felt terribly awkward, but the dream was more important than mere social discomfort. They stopped talking when they saw him, and before they had a chance to start giggling, he plunged in breathlessly. "Francine, I . . . I've got to ask you something. Could . . . could I see you alone for a minute?"

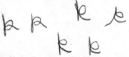

The girls' eyes widened, and they looked significantly at one another. Francine said, "Well, maybe I don't feel like talking to you."

"Oh, but Francine, it's . . ." He looked at the other girls and blushed. "You know it's not . . . not anything personal or anything. You know what it's about. I've just got to . . ." His voice trailed off.

She sighed. "Oh, all right. See you later, kids." She started off down the street. "Come on, Paul."

Walking beside her, he didn't know how to begin. She glanced up at him, then looked back at the other girls. "Lord knows how I'm going to explain this to them," she muttered.

"Francine," Paul said, "you said something about rescuing a kid. Are you talking about that little white figure that's running toward the glowing thing?"

"Sure," she said calmly. "It's a little kid and he doesn't know what he's doing and in a minute something terrible is going to happen to him. And I . . . I mean *we* . . . have to save him. Couldn't you figure that out?"

"But . . ." Paul tried to ignore her scornful tone, "I couldn't see so clearly that it was a little kid. But what do you think is the dangerous part? That creature he's running away from, or the glowing thing he's running toward?"

"I'm not sure," she said. "But I kind of think the glowing thing is scarier."

"What about the word *Stardust* over that building?" Paul said. "What do you think that means?"

"What word?" She turned and faced him. "I see the building, but no word over it."

Now it was his turn to be superior. "Can't you remember any—?" he began, but when he saw her face start to harden again, he cut himself short. "From where I am, I can see a funny low building off to the left, with these letters over it that say *Stardust*. But you don't see the letters, right?"

"Uh uh." She shook her head, her mouth half-open.

"Now that *is* strange," Paul said. They were both standing still and staring at each other. "You can tell it's a little kid, and I can't," he went on, musing. "And I see the letters and you don't. I wonder if there are any other differences, or if everything else is exactly the same."

"Maybe we should each just tell everything we see— *everything*," Francine suggested.

"Okay," said Paul. And walking slowly through the pale spring sunlight, they proceeded to describe to each other in complete detail the dream as each of them experienced it. The only other difference they could find had to do with the murmuring voices. They both heard them, but only Paul had noticed that one word, *jaleela*, was repeated more often than anything else. They both agreed that the most important part was the sense of danger, of imminent catastrophe, that only they could avert.

"And it's not just going to affect the little kid, *we're* in danger too," Francine insisted. "I don't know what it is, but it's completely horrible."

"I know," Paul agreed, and he shivered in spite of himself.

He was paying no attention to where they were going, only seeing the dream in his mind, until Francine stopped walking and said, "Well, here we are. This is my block."

Paul blinked and looked around. They were standing on a street corner in a neighborhood he did not know, quite different from his own. The street was lined with three-decker wooden apartment houses, all exactly the same except for varying degrees of disrepair, all very close together. There were no trees or yards, only cracked sidewalks and an occasional patch of dirt in front of one of the houses.

"Oh," Paul said. He was surprised that Francine lived in a neighborhood like this, but he tried not to show it. "Well, um, I guess . . . I wonder what we should do?"

She shrugged, and her previous attitude toward him returned. "What's there to do?" she said casually. "Just . . . maybe we'll figure something out."

"Oh, sure. Is that where you live?" he asked her vaguely, pointing to a house on the other side of the street and several houses down from where they were standing.

"Yeah." She sounded surprised. "How did you know it was that one?"

"I don't know. It just seemed like it." He paused. "Well, um, I guess I'll go. Could you . . . ." He was embarrassed again. "How do I get back to school?"

14

She pointed out the way and he hurried off, eager to get away from her dreary neighborhood and back to his own. It was good to shake off the shabby uncomfortable feeling that her environment and her manner had produced in him, and he did not look back to see her standing there, staring after him with an unusually thoughtful expression on her face.

That night in the dream, he saw Francine clearly. She moved slowly beside him, her hair blown back from her face by the wind, staring at the glowing sphere and the running child. She seemed different in the dream, resourceful and strong. He felt no distaste for her at all, only the intense longing to reach out to her, to join with her and run toward the events in the center of the field.

There were other changes too. He could tell now that the figure in white was a little boy with black hair. He could even see the expression on his face—happy, entranced—as he gamboled in his white pajamas around the glowing, changing sphere, oblivious to the terrible menace that was about to engulf them all. Behind him lumbered the dark creature, still indistinct, but behaving differently now, for occasionally it would turn toward Paul and Francine, shaking its body in an odd manner.

The terror and the urgency rolled over them now like great black waves, the voices babbled hysterically, and the humming noise rose to a penetrating scream. And then just as Paul started to run, there was a sickening

lurch, the ground vanished beneath his feet as he pitched forward into inky blackness, and the scream was coming from his own throat.

When he awoke, he was more terrified than ever before. As he lay there trembling in the darkness, his first reaction was an urgent need to talk to Francine, thinking of her as she was in the dream. But then he remembered what she was like at school, and he felt the same old reluctance to have anything to do with her.

He made no effort to talk to her next day. Instead of staying in the classroom during recess, as he usually did, he went to a secret little courtyard that he knew about at the side of the school building, in an attempt to keep away from her. Yet somehow she managed to find him there—as part of him had been hoping she would. She approached him rather hesitantly. Her manner, however, was still hostile when she announced, "It was different last night, wasn't it."

He nodded, feeling irritated by the sound of her voice.

She seemed to sense his mood, and shuffled her feet uncomfortably. "The whole thing was closer, and I could see you better."

"I could see you," he interrupted. "For the first time I could see you too."

"And I could see those letters over the building, *Stardust*. I never saw them at all, until I talked to you. So I was thinking about it, and—"

He interrupted her again, confident that whatever

she had to say would not be important. "And those things changed so suddenly, right after you and I found out about each other and told each other what we knew. We made contact, and that brought us farther into the dream. We could see everything better."

"That's just what I was going to say, if you'd given me the chance."

"You were?"

"Yeah," she said dryly.

"But listen," he went on quickly, not wanting to believe that he had underestimated her. "I thought of something else. Something really important. You knew something that—"

"I know what you're going to say," she said matter-of-factly. "You're going to say how we each knew something the other didn't know, and when we told each other, it helped us to get deeper into the dream. And if we find that little kid, and find out what he knows, then we'll get even deeper into it, and then maybe we'll be able to save him and ourselves. Right?"

Paul was amazed. "But . . . but how did you know that was exactly what I was going to say?"

She seemed a bit surprised herself. "I don't know how I knew. I just knew," she said slowly. For a moment they were both silent. Then she tossed her head and her brusque manner returned. "So go on," she said crisply.

"Go on? What do you mean?"

"I mean tell me that really important idea you had."

"But that was it. To find the little kid."

"Some idea!" she said. "Did you ever think about how we're going to find him, brain boy? Out of all the people in the world, how are we going to find him? You're supposed to be so smart, why don't you answer that one?"

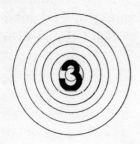

She was right, of course. Finding her had been so easy (it was she, in fact, who had found him, he admitted grudgingly to himself) that he had not even thought about the problem of finding the essential third person. Somehow he had just assumed that it would happen on its own. But now his brief elation and confidence were swept away by the hopelessness of the situation, and he did not even answer her.

She was still fuming. "Yeah," she said. "Sure you don't know what to do. And me, I was stupid enough to think maybe you'd have an idea." She stared straight ahead. "Wow, whoever's running this show really threw me in with a winner, that's for sure. I wish I could forget about the whole stupid thing."

"Then why don't you?" he said petulantly, feeling wounded.

" 'Then why don't you?' " she mimicked. "Yeah, sure I'm going to forget it. Sure I'm going to forget that . . . that feeling." And as she said the word, her voice dropped.

"That feeling of something about to happen, you mean?" he asked her, forgetting to be wounded as the icy sensation flowed between them, the dark and threatening power of it suddenly seeming to fill the courtyard, as though something had blotted out the sunlight. "It was worse last night, wasn't it," he said in the sudden ominous silence.

"Oh, it was bad," Francine murmured in a hushed voice, shaking her head. "I don't know what it is, but it's worse than anything I ever . . . and we're the ones who have to do something about it."

"I know," he agreed. "I can't think about anything else. We've got to find that kid."

"Yeah." She pushed her hair back and looked away. "Yeah, right back to the beginning again," she said in her normal voice. "Oh, why isn't this happening with somebody who . . ."

"Well, personally I don't know what makes you think *you're* such a great person to be in it with," said Paul, in an uncharacteristic burst of anger. "You never do anything except whisper and giggle and—"

"Yeah? *Teacher's pet!*" she said, her voice rising as she backed away. "I'm going back now, so nobody will see me with *you*." And she hurried out of the courtyard.

They did not speak to each other again that day. Paul was miserable and furious. When he got home he sulked in his room, and once again did no homework. Why did he need Francine? It was probably a mistake; she wasn't really in the dream. Just forget about her, he told himself as he got into bed. You can do it on your own.

He awoke several hours later, shuddering and shaken and dripping with sweat, only barely managing to keep himself from crying out in anguish. The unknown disaster was coming faster, and it was unimaginably terrible. His antipathy toward Francine paled in comparison. There was no alternative but to join with her and do whatever it was they had to do to avert the terror.

There was no need even to ask her about it. She was jumpy and frightened when she joined him at recess, and there were dark rings under her eyes. He could tell exactly how she felt before she said a word. "Maybe we should skip the rest of the day," she said tensely. It was Friday afternoon. "Just skip and start looking for him right now!"

"Oh, we can't," said Paul. "I'm already in trouble as it is. Tomorrow is Saturday. We'll have to wait until then."

"But even then, what can we do then?" There was a frantic edge to her voice. "Where do we look? Where do we go? What are we even looking *for*?"

"I don't know, I don't know! But what else can we do? Just go everywhere and keep looking for the right person. He's probably looking for us too."

"Yeah, that's right," Francine said a little more calmly. "Maybe that does make sense."

Paul did manage to do some homework that evening, not only to keep Miss Keck at bay, but also to try to keep his mind occupied and to put off the moment when he had to go to bed. He was so anxious and apprehensive about the terror of the dream now, that it seemed as though sleep would be impossible. Unfortunately, it was not.

The dream was changing again. As the terror increased, certain things faded away and others came to take their place. *Stardust* was hardly noticeable now. Instead, he was aware of the moon, a full moon hanging above them like a pale echo of the dazzling, shimmering globe in the middle of the field. The little boy was rapt, in a trance; the creature behind had almost reached him now. The high-pitched whining rose and fell, the eerie babble of voices, and as the horror bore down upon him he suddenly noticed other lights at the edge of the field, swinging and swirling in unlikely arcs, tied inextricably to the terrible event that they somehow had to prevent.

Paul and Francine walked for hours and hours the next day, looking for the little boy. Eyes, noses, mouths, endless combinations of different features, and none of them seemed right. "And how do we even know he's in the city?" said Francine. "Or even in this country?"

"We don't know," said Paul. "But what else can we do? Fly around the world?"

A few minutes later, on a busy street corner, Francine suddenly stopped walking. "Hey!" she cried out. "We're making a big mistake."

People were pushing past impatiently, and two men behind almost bumped into them. Paul pulled Francine over to the side and said, "Okay, what is it?"

"Well," she said a little breathlessly, "here we are doing this impossible thing of looking for this kid, but we haven't even stopped to think about what the dream really *is*, what it means, and why it's happening to *us*. It's like we're doing the whole thing backwards."

"Huh," said Paul, feeling disappointed because her idea was so obviously right and he had not thought of it, but at the same time excited by the possibilities it offered.

"I mean," Francine went on, "there must be something about us, about you and about me, that's the same; otherwise, we both wouldn't be having the same dream. If we find out what it is, there's got to be some kind of answer there."

"I . . . I guess you're right," Paul said. "How come I didn't think of that?"

"Beats me, brain boy," Francine said, smiling slightly. "Maybe because you could never stand to think anything about us *could* be the same."

"Oh, well," said Paul, irritated that she had read his mind so accurately. (How had she been able to do it?) "Let's just go sit down somewhere and try to figure this all out."

They repaired to a booth in a nearby soda fountain.

Francine ordered a huge banana split and a Coke. Paul had french fries.

"Ugh, french fries," said Francine. "Who ever just gets french fries?"

"I can't stand ice cream," Paul said, as the waitress set a gooey overflowing bowl in front of Francine and a small plate in front of him.

"Well," said Francine, digging in, "that isn't the thing that's the same about us, that's for sure."

"But I wonder what it could be?" Paul said, thoughtfully munching a french fry. "We do seem pretty different. How are we ever going to figure it out?" He paused for a moment. "Well, one thing is, both our parents are divorced, and we live with our mothers."

Francine almost dropped her spoon. "How did you know that about me?"

"I . . . . I don't know how I knew," Paul said, just as surprised as she was. "It just kind of popped into my head, and then I said it without even thinking about it."

"Wow, that's weird," she said slowly. "I don't tell anybody about that. My best friend, Sally, is the only one who knows. Did she tell you?"

"You know she never talks to me," said Paul. "I don't know how I knew," he repeated, and then they just stared at each other across the table until Paul, embarrassed, let his eyes flicker back to the french fries.

"Well, anyway," Francine said finally, "that's one thing that's the same, but it doesn't seem to have much to do with the dream. There must be something else." She took a sip of her Coke and crunched a few pieces of ice, a sound Paul couldn't stand. "It's probably something weird. What's the weirdest thing that ever happened to you?"

"Once I was in an airplane and it hit an air pocket and fell a hundred feet in one second and I bumped my head on the ceiling. Those breathing things came down and everything. It was horrible."

"Well, that never happened to me," said Francine, crunching more ice. "But once I was trapped in an elevator. We were stuck there for half an hour. It was real crowded and people got hysterical. One fat lady fainted and fell right on top of me."

"Hmmm," said Paul. "Well, I guess that doesn't get us anywhere."

"Well, we'll just have to keep trying," she said, beginning to crunch more ice and then quickly stopping. "Sorry, I know you can't stand that sound."

"That's right!" said Paul, leaning forward suddenly. "But *how* did you know?"

"I . . ." She seemed puzzled. "I don't know. It's like I just suddenly remembered it or something. But I know you never told me that."

Paul slowly shook his head. "Now that is something I call weird."

"It's as if . . . sometimes we can tell what the other one is thinking," Francine murmured. "It keeps happening."

And at last Paul had a brilliant idea of his own. "Maybe that's what the dream is," he said, "Maybe it's somebody else, calling out for help by sending us the dream, and somehow we can get the message. Because we have—"

"Because . . . because we have REM, or whatever it is," Francine finished in a hushed voice.

"ESP. Extrasensory perception. Mental telepathy," he corrected her, slowly sitting back in his seat. He knew his mother would say that it didn't exist. Yet hadn't they just had direct proof that they could read one another's minds? It wasn't that he could hear her thoughts as words, exactly; just that somehow, sometimes he seemed to be able to tell what she was thinking—and she could tell what he was thinking. It was an exciting feeling, of course, even though he still wasn't sure he really believed in it. But it was also awesome, even frightening. He wasn't sure he really wanted to believe in it.

"But why is it happening to *us*?" Francine sounded frightened too. "Why is the person sending the dream to us? And if it really is true, then what made us like this?"

"I have no idea," said Paul, feeling shaky all over, as though his mother had just screamed at him.

"Well, we'll just have to find out," Francine said, all at once sounding brisk again. "We'll just have to tell each other everything, starting from the day we were born. If there's any clue or any connection, that's the way to find it."

It proved to be quite a lengthy, as well as frustrating, process. Paul had trouble concentrating, because he kept wondering if he really did have ESP and thinking how unreal it seemed. They were still on their infancies when they had to leave the drugstore because other people were waiting to sit down. The two men who had been sitting in the booth next to theirs had to leave too.

"Then they moved my father to another army base," Francine was saying as they strolled down the street. "So we had to move again, this time to Stockton, California. We lived in a crazy old house in the desert, and I used to pick on the kid who lived downstairs. Were you ever there? . . . Paul? Are you listening?"

"What? Oh, sorry. What did you just say?"

"Stockton, California!" she said furiously and stamped her foot. "Paul, we are never going to get anywhere if you won't pay attention."

"But I can't help it," he said. "I just . . . I can't stop thinking about having mental telepathy. I guess it must be true, but still, it's so hard to believe. And if it is true, it's a big deal; it's a huge deal; it's probably the most important thing that will ever happen to us!"

She grabbed him by the arm and pulled him around to face her. "Well, the dream is a big deal too; the dream is important!" she shouted. "Come on, Paul!"

"Oh, all right," he said, feeling guilty and irritated. "But I already told you, I've never been out West, and you only moved here a year ago, and nothing weird happened in the last year, so it all seems sort of hopeless and—" Suddenly he stopped. "Wait a minute," he went on slowly.

"What?" said Francine. "What? Go on, go on!"

"I did go out West once, with my mother, when she

was getting the divorce. We were in Nevada for about six weeks. How could I forget it?"

"Because it was probably horrible and you didn't want to remember it," said Francine with another surprising flash of intuition. "But when was it? Do you remember when you were there?"

"Let's see," he said, counting on his fingers. "It must have been . . . yes, it was four years ago last summer. It'll be five years this summer. I think it was in July, so it's five years ago this coming July."

"Well, we never lived in Nevada," said Francine, "But I'm sure we were there a couple of times, going from one place to another. Maybe you and I were there at the same time; maybe something happened when we were there that we don't know about or don't remember."

"But it seems so distant from—"

"Look, Paul," she said as though she were talking to a small boy, "it's the only thing we have to go on. Now you go home and ask your mother exactly when you were there, and where you were, and if anything funny happened. And I'll ask mine. And then call me and we'll try to figure it out. Okay?"

"Sure," he said, uncomfortable with her now.

"Okay," she said. "See you." And she turned and walked away from him.

On the way home, Paul thought about how unlucky he was to have mental telepathy with Francine. It was such an exciting thing to happen, and yet Francine ruined it. He no longer really considered her silly. Instead, she gave him the feeling that *he* was dull or inferior in some way. It was a difficult feeling to tolerate. What was he doing that made her feel that way? What was he doing wrong?

His mother did indeed remember Nevada. "I had to waste six weeks of my life in that place," she said, and she emphatically sliced through an onion.

"But do you remember when it was? I mean what the exact dates were?"

"I suppose I could if I had to." She looked up at him from the cutting board. "But why do you want to know?"

"I don't know." Behind his back he cracked his knuckles, though he was attempting to appear calm and almost indifferent to the questions he was asking. "It's just that I hardly remember being there. It seems funny to go someplace and then hardly remember being there at all. Do you remember where we stayed?"

"Oh, it was just outside of Reno. I can't remember exactly."

He prepared himself to ask the question that he knew would blow his cover and bring on a torrent of questions from her. He let his fingers run casually through the pages of a cookbook lying open on the kitchen counter. "When we were there," he said slowly, "did anything . . . do you remember if anything sort of weird or—"

But she interrupted him with a little laugh before he

had a chance to ask it. "What I won't forget is the name of the motel where we stayed," she said, and looked away from him. "That sign flashed outside my window all night. Stardust. The Stardust Motel."

"Hello."

"Hello. Is Francine there?"

"Who's calling?"

It occurred to Paul at this moment that mental telepathy could be a really practical advantage, if he and Francine could strengthen it and get it more under their control. "Uh . . . my name is Paul. I'm in Francine's class at school. I just wanted to find out what the assignment was."

"On a Saturday night you're asking Francine what the assignment is?"

He heard a muffled disturbance in the background, then Francine's voice on the line. "Paul?"

"Yes, it's me."

"Did you—" Then she said, away from the receiver, "Ma, it's only Paul, from school. We're doing a project together." He heard footsteps and a door closing. "Paul? Did you ask her?"

"Yes. We were there from July second to August thirteenth."

"Well, we *were* in Nevada that July, too, just like I thought. July eleventh to eighteenth. My mother also remembers the place where we stayed." There was silence.

Paul didn't want to tell her the name of the motel. After all, it was he who had seen the word first in the dream; it might have been an unconscious memory on his part. Only if Francine's mother came up with the same name would the coincidence be significant. "Where did you stay?" he asked her.

"The Stardust Motel," Francine said.

After a moment, during which Paul listened to his heartbeat speed up dramatically and then gradually begin to slow down, he said, "Well, I guess . . . I guess it really is a pretty amazing coincidence that we were both there the same week. But it still doesn't mean that—"

"Did you ask her if anything weird happened?" Francine asked quickly.

"Yes." Paul sighed. "First she wanted to know what I meant by *weird*, then she wanted to know why I wanted to know, then she wanted to know if I was unhappy not living with my father. It went on and on, just like I knew it would." He looked behind himself to make sure the kitchen door was closed.

"But did she remember anything weird?" Francine said impatiently.

"No. She just said it was boring and a waste of time."

"Yeah. Well mine didn't remember anything either. I guess we're going to have to find out ourselves."

"But how are we going to find out? I mean, who else would know if—"

"You're supposed to be the smart one," she said, her words rapid, her voice high-pitched through the tele-phone. "Figure it out. I have to get off now or my mother will get suspicious. See you on Monday."

For a moment he just stood there with the receiver in his hand, rankling once more at her implication that he was slow, that he put a damper on things, that he was incompetent. The worst part of it was that he was almost beginning to believe her. Francine, who was always so giggly and stupid, making *him* feel inferior! Yet it really was Francine who had most of the ideas and who always seemed to know what to do. This time, he decided, he would prove that she was wrong. He would find out—on his own—what, if anything, had happened in Reno, Nevada, the week of July 11 to 18.

He realized, as he brushed his teeth, that it probably wouldn't even be so very difficult. All he would have to do was find the newspapers from that particular week. There must be lots of them in the main branch of the public library.

He got into bed. In the darkness he could see the

moon outside his window. In the dream it's a full moon, he thought drowsily, trying to prepare himself for what was about to happen. Now it's bigger than a half moon. I wonder if it means anything. I wonder if something's going to happen when the moon gets full. . . .

As he sank into sleep, the moon seemed to change and grow, until it had become a full moon hanging over the field. Beside him stood Francine, staring straight ahead, her hair blown back. Around them tingled the strange vibrations, the high-pitched whining that rose and fell. Around them the voices whispered and sang, "Come here, come here. . . . Not that way, Cookie, Cookie, jaleela, jaleela . . . I want you. . . ." It seemed almost as if the ground were trembling, and Paul felt the nervousness begin inside him as the unearthly, throbbing sphere appeared over the center of the field. Even though he had been through the dream many times now, there was always a disorienting uncertainty about how it was going to end. For each time, there was the possibility that the terrible thing might happen before they had a chance to prevent it.

The ominous lights at the edges of the field were swinging closer now—that was where the danger lay; and tonight he realized that they were moving toward them. He turned to Francine, trying to get her to hurry, but he could not speak; he could barely move. The struggle and frustration he was going through were also evident in the wrinkles of tension around Francine's eyes and the hard line of her mouth. If only they could go faster!

Then Francine looked again toward the center of the field, and his eyes followed hers. The little boy in white was skipping toward the suspended sphere, enraptured and smiling, drawn trancelike by its pulsating glow and oblivious to the large black thing loping behind him. Oblivious also to the menacing pinpoints of light hovering closer and closer. *Run, Francine, run!* Paul thought at her frantically as the lights swung toward them; and suddenly in a tremendous whirl of wind and sound, they *were* running. There was a dizzying rush of images, as the little boy's smiling face swam close to them, and the strange black creature, which was now somehow familiar, and the swirling lights and a chorus of voices shrieking madly, and then it was too late, he knew it was too late, and he was plunging down, down, down . . .

"Well, did you find anything out yet?" Francine asked him at recess on Monday.

"How could I? The library was closed yesterday."

"What does the library have to do with anything?"

"Because," he explained with exaggerated patience, "the library is where they have newspapers and things that will say if anything unusual happened in Reno, Nevada, between July eleventh and eighteenth. Can you think of any other way to start trying to find out?"

"No. I guess that makes sense," she admitted. "I just hope it doesn't take too long. That dream is getting so . . . bad."

. "Well, I'm going right after school today," he said.

Part of him wanted to maintain a certain superior reserve with Francine, because he still felt hurt by her attitude. The intensity of the dream overruled his pride, however, and he added, "It's weird the way it keeps changing and getting worse. It's almost like it's telling us the horrible thing is going to happen anyway, no matter what we do."

"I know," Francine said, biting her lip nervously. "But it's still so . . . . obscure. The meaning isn't getting any clearer."

"Well, the only thing is . . . did you notice the moon?"

"I guess so. What about it?"

"In the dream it's a full moon. Maybe that means that the thing—whatever it is—is going to happen when there's a full moon."

"When's the next full moon?" she asked him, her voice rising slightly.

"It looks pretty big now. I guess it will be full in a few days."

"Oh, we have to hurry," she said fervently. "I'm going with you to the library today."

Francine looked around uncertainly as they entered the main hall of the old library, and in his head Paul caught a brief flash of her discomfort and unfamiliarity with the place. "This way," he said briskly, and led her without hesitating across the echoing marble floor, past the main staircase, and down a narrow hallway to the left.

"Where are we going?" she whispered behind him.

"To the periodicals room, of course," he said, enjoying the satisfaction of being able to show her around.

The satisfaction vanished, however, when they reached the entrance to the periodicals section and the woman behind the desk informed them that the stacks were closed.

"Closed?" Paul said. "But they never used to be closed before."

"It's a new policy," the woman said. "When the stacks were open, people left everything out of order, and too many old newspapers and magazines were disappearing. Now you fill out these request slips and wait until someone on the staff finds the material you want and brings it up here."

"But . . . but what if you don't know which newspaper you want?"

"You look it up in the catalogue," the woman said, turning back to her work.

They stepped out into the hallway. "Now what do we do?" Francine whispered.

"It's so stupid!" Paul said angrily. "You used to be able to just go down there and browse around. How are we ever going to find out what we want from the catalogue?"

"You're the one that's supposed to know your way around here," said Francine. "Don't ask me what to do."

"I wasn't asking you," he said, feeling inferior and frustrated all over again. He looked back into the periodicals department. The librarian had left her desk and was puttering around in the reading room behind it. An idea occurred to Paul. But did he have the nerve? He glanced at Francine's face and decided that he did. "Come on," he whispered. "Hurry!" He darted back toward the desk.

"But she said—"

"Shhh!"

To the left of the desk was a tiny elevator. He pressed the button. The doors slid open noisily, but the librarian, at the other end of the room, did not turn around. Paul pulled Francine inside and pushed the basement button.

The elevator rattled and quivered as they descended. Paul was nervous about sneaking in, of course. But he did not even need to look at Francine to know that she was impressed. That made the risk worthwhile.

They emerged into a maze of dark narrow corridors. Paul knew these corridors well, and in a minute he had found the appropriate section. He began searching quickly, aware that someone might appear at any moment and throw them out. Francine was not much help, hovering behind him and reading over his shoulder in the half-darkness; but at least her behavior helped him to feel superior.

Still, it was rather disheartening to have to read through endless pages as the minute hand on his wristwatch spun around, not finding any mention of Reno, Nevada. Finally Francine stopped looking over his shoulder and began pouring through different periodicals on her own, and a very short time later he heard her say, "Hey, Paul, listen to this!"

"What?" he said, his heart beginning to pound. He was excited, of course, that she had found something, but also disappointed that it had not been he.

" 'Las Vegas, Nevada, July 12,' " she read slowly. " 'An 18-month-old baby girl won $650 at a slot machine here today, with one nickel. The child's mother, Mrs. Godfrey Bisbane, said, "Sheila just wandered away, and when I found her she was standing there with silver dollars pouring down all over her." One bystander said that—' "

"Oh, Francine!" said Paul, suddenly extremely irritated. "Who cares? I thought you'd found something. We don't have time to read everything. Somebody might come down here any minute and throw us out. Don't you know how to skim?" It was particularly annoying because he had been making an intense effort to skip over everything that didn't seem related to their search, and had thereby been denying himself all sorts of interesting tidbits.

"I just thought it was interesting," she said, pouting. "You don't have to be so grouchy."

"Yes, but it's almost five now, and we'll have to leave soon and go through another night without knowing any more than before."

"Oh, you're right, you're right," she said, and began looking harder than ever.

He needn't have worried, however. Fifteen minutes later he found himself staring, almost in disbelief, at exactly the piece of information they were looking for. "Oh, no," he said softly, slowly standing up as he read. "Oh, no, this is incredible." The excitement was bubbling up through his body in tingling electric waves. "This is it, Francine," he said, not thinking about the librarian, his voice rising almost to a shout. "Francine, this is it!"

"What?" she said. "What is it, Paul?" forgetting to whisper in her excitement and, in fact, practically shouting herself.

"Just *listen* to this." And he began to read. " 'Reno, Nevada, July 15. An unidentified—' "

"What are you children doing here?" said the librarian, who had suddenly materialized beside them. "I thought I told you the stacks were closed."

Francine jumped. "Oh!" she said. "But we just found . . . Please, just let us stay another minute so he can read this thing to me."

"This is just the kind of behavior we are trying to prevent," said the librarian. "Put that volume away this instant and go back upstairs."

Paul did not move or speak, but stood there reading rapidly, occasionally gasping to himself.

"Didn't you hear me?" said the librarian. "You are not allowed down here! If you don't leave right away, I'll have to ask the guard to—"

"Okay," said Paul, slamming the volume shut and shoving it back onto the shelf. "Bye. See you later. Come on, Francine."

"Paul, what *was* it?" Francine asked him as the elevator door slid shut.

Neither of them moved to push the button. If Paul had not been so excited, he might have prolonged the suspense; but as it was, he could barely get the words

42

out fast enough. "Francine, there was a UFO there on July fifteenth."

"What are you talking about? What's a UFO?"

"Unidentified flying object. Supposedly from outer space."

"Paul, are you trying to kid me?"

"No, not at all. Every once in a while people claim to see weird flying things, like flying saucers and stuff. And I never believed it before; I always just assumed that the people were crazy; but now . . ."

"Go on! Go on!"

"Well, on the night of July fifteenth, a woman claimed to see a glowing sphere floating over the earth in the middle of a field. Sound familiar?"

"Paul, you're making this up!"

"I'm *not*, Francine. It was all in the paper. A glowing sphere, just like in the dream. The woman who saw it said she felt vibrations coming from it. And her name was . . ." He was so excited now that he could hardly say it. "Her name was *Mrs. Diana Jaleela,* and she was staying at the Stardust Motel."

At that moment the elevator began its quivering ascent. Someone above had pushed the button, but they were both too excited to pay any attention to it.

"Anyway, this Mrs. Jaleela was in her room and she saw something out the window, so she went outside to look. Right in back of the motel was a field, and in the middle of it was the sphere. Mrs. Jaleela got her dog and went to look closer at it. Her dog's name was . . . Now what was her dog's name?"

44

"Oh, who cares what her dog's name was!" cried Francine, as the door opened and two men got into the elevator. Paul and Francine ignored them completely. "Who cares what her dumb dog's name was! Just go on!"

"Rose," Paul said. "Her dog's name was Rose. Anyway, so she went a little closer to the glowing thing. And then she noticed a humming noise coming from it, and Rose starting snarling. Francine, do you know what that means?"

"Just go on!" Francine shouted at him.

"That's all," Paul said. "When she heard the noise she turned and ran back to her room, and so did Rose. And then she called the police. But when the police got there, the thing was gone. Francine, of course you realize what this means! It's so amazing I can hardly stand it!"

Francine and Paul just stared at each other. The elevator had returned to the basement, and the door slid open, revealing the librarian.

She stepped backwards. "What . . . what are you people doing on this elevator?" she said. "And you two children again! What do I have to do to keep you—"

But she didn't have a chance to finish because Francine pushed the button and the door slid shut in the middle of her sentence. Paul was still hardly aware of anything but his story, though he did begin speaking in an undertone. "What it means is that the UFO was probably radiating some kind of telepathic beam. And you and I were in the motel and we got some of it. But

Mrs. Jaleela got the most. It means about a million things."

"It's so amazing how perfectly it ties up with the dream," Francine murmured. "Are you *sure* you're not making it—"

"I am *not* making it up!" Paul insisted. "We can come back tomorrow and you can read it yourself."

The elevator had arrived again at the main floor. "Come on, let's get off this thing," said Francine, and she pulled Paul out of the elevator. They hurried back to the front lobby.

"It's just so amazing," Paul said. "I can still hardly—"

"Well, the first thing we have to do is find this Mrs. Jaleela," said Francine, practically.

"But . . . where is she?" said Paul, who was still in a kind of daze. "Who knows where she is?"

"I know the first place to look," said Francine, and she headed for a bank of phone booths at the back of the lobby.

"But she couldn't possibly live here, in the same city as us," said Paul, following her. "That would be just too much of a—"

"But we might as well look," said Francine, already pawing through the phone book chained inside the first booth. "Let's see now . . . Does *J* come before *O*?" And then it was Francine's turn to gasp to herself.

"Is it there?" Paul asked her breathlessly.

"Jaleela Diana," Francine read in an awed voice. "143 Colgate. 237-4586." She dropped the phone book and looked at him. "Should we call her up?"

"But that's fantastic," said Paul. "It's so amazing that she's here too, if she's the same one. Uh . . . maybe we should wait before we call her. I mean, we should discuss it and figure out what we're going to say."

At last Francine seemed to believe the story and to be as thrilled about it as Paul was. They hurried out of the library and started home, too excited to notice the slight drizzle, or the fact that they were shouting at each other, or the curious looks of passersby. They were also too excited to notice that the two men who had been with them on the elevator had followed them out of the library, and were now following them home.

5

"Hello."

"Hello. Is Mrs. Jaleela there?"

"Speaking."

"Oh. Mrs. Jaleela, my name is Francine Gill. I'm doing this project for school with a friend. We go to the Wiley School. And we're doing this project about . . . about UFOs. And um, we read an article about how you saw one once, an unidentified flying object . . ."

"Go on, go on!" Paul whispered fiercely.

"And we were wondering if maybe we could interview you about it some time," Francine said in one breath.

"Oh," said Mrs. Jaleela. There was a long silence.

"What's she saying? What's she saying?" Paul whispered.

"Shhhhh!" Francine said to him, her hand over the mouthpiece. Then she said into the phone, "Mrs. Jaleela? Are you there, Mrs. Jaleela?"

"Oh," said Mrs. Jaleela, her voice sounding vague and scratchy over the phone. "That was so long ago. I don't really remember it very well."

"Well, Mrs. Jaleela," Francine said, "We don't want to invade your privacy or anything." (Paul was rather surprised by how grown-up she sounded.) "But we don't have any firsthand information in our report. It would really make a big difference to us and we would appreciate it very much."

"How old are you?" Mrs. Jaleela asked her slowly.

"We're both twelve."

"And it's just two of you?"

"Yes. Me and my—friend, Paul."

"And you wouldn't bring anyone else with you?"

"No."

"Uh . . ." It seemed as though Mrs. Jaleela was trying to think of another question. "What's your teacher's name?"

"Miss Keck."

"Well . . ." There was another long silence. "Well, all right. When would you like to come over?"

"Oh, any time that's all right with you."

"Well . . . How about tomorrow afternoon? Around four?"

"Oh, that would be fine, Mrs. Jaleela," said Francine. "That would be perfect. Thank you very much. See you tomorrow."

"Tomorrow?" Paul demanded, dragging Francine out of the booth almost before she had a chance to hang up the phone. "She'll see us tomorrow?"

"Yes. We're going over to her house at four."

"Fantastic!" he said, clasping his hands together. He felt so elated that he added, "You were good, Francine. She seemed scared, but you sounded very harmless and sincere."

Francine looked at him rather warily. "You . . . you must have got that from telepathy. She *was* scared, and *harmless* and *sincere* were the exact words in my mind. In fact . . . I was *trying* to send those words to her."

"And I got them," Paul murmured.

"I wonder if she did too?" said Francine.

"Maybe we can find out tomorrow," said Paul. "I wonder how much she knows?"

The newspaper article had certainly answered some questions. Now at least part of the dream could be explained: *Stardust*, the field, and the glowing sphere. It also seemed logical that their gift of communication had come from that experience, though how far it went, and what they could really do with it, they still did not know.

They also did not know who, if anybody, was sending them the dream, or the significance of the little boy and the creature loping behind him. And they still had no answer to the most important questions—what was the danger that was approaching, when was it going to come, and what, if anything, could the two of them do about it. Mrs. Jaleela, they hoped, would have some answers for them.

They were both quiet the next day when they started out for Mrs. Jaleela's house. But after a few blocks, Francine said, "I wonder if we'll ever know where that UFO thing came from."

"I guess there's no way we can find out what it was, or where it was sent from," Paul said. "All we know is that it probably didn't come from the Earth and that it did something to our brains so we can sort of tell what each other is thinking—and what the person who's sending us the dream is thinking. And maybe there's something dangerous about it too, but so far, I think it's great to have mental telepathy."

"Yeah, but what good has it done us?" said Francine, practical as usual. "So far it's only been a drag."

"Well, we just never tried to do anything with it," said Paul. "I mean, it always happens inadvertently, without our control. I think maybe we should experiment with it, fool around a little bit and see what we can really do."

"Like how?" said Francine, beginning to sound interested.

"Let me think about it," said Paul. He had noticed earlier that there were two very ordinary-looking men about half a block behind them on the quiet residential street. Now he began thinking about them, concentrating on them as hard as he could, and willing Francine to turn around and notice them.

In about thirty seconds Francine turned around and

looked at the two men. "Don't those two men behind us look familiar?" she said.

"It works!" Paul cried out, and gave a little excited hop.

"*What* works?"

"I was thinking hard about those two men and trying to get you to turn around and look at them. And then you did! What did it feel like?"

"Well . . ." She thought for a moment. "Actually, it was strange, because I hadn't noticed them at all. Then I got a vague picture of two figures, and an itchy feeling like I should turn around. And I did and there they were." She was staring at Paul, her eyes wide. "That's really what you were thinking?"

"Yes," Paul said, feeling terribly excited. "Now you try one."

"But don't they look familiar?" Francine said, turning briefly to look at the two men again.

"Who? Oh, the two men? But how could they look familiar?" said Paul impatiently. "They look just like a thousand other people you see every day. Now you think of something."

"But I have a feeling I've seen them somewhere before. Maybe they're following us."

"Oh, you're just imagining things," Paul said with irritation. "They're completely ordinary looking. Come on, think of something."

He tried to open his mind as Francine walked beside him, her face tightened with concentration. Then a picture of a small doll standing under a bright silvery spray flashed into his head. "You're not thinking of . . . a doll standing in the shower, are you?" he asked her.

"Well," said Francine, "what I was thinking about was the baby in Las Vegas who won at the slot machine—the one that I read about in the paper the other day. I guess it didn't come through too clear."

"Were you concentrating really hard?"

"As hard as I could!" she said defensively. "It seems like we really do have it, but we just don't have it very strong."

"Well, we just have to practice more, that's all," Paul insisted. "I know we can get better at it if we work on it." He thought for a moment. "The other thing is, we were both thinking of things the other one already knew about and could have remembered. We should try it with something completely crazy that the other one never heard of. I'll try one."

"Wait a minute," said Francine. She stopped walking. "This is Colgate. We better start looking for the house."

It was a small brick apartment house on the corner of a block that consisted mostly of private homes. There were six buzzers in the tiny dark lobby. All the names beside them were printed, except for *D. Jaleela*, which was written out in a rather shaky hand. "Is it the right time?" Paul whispered.

"Just after four."

"And we're sure we know what we're going to say?"

"Just that we're doing a report and we saw her name in that newspaper article. We can't say anything else at

53

first, because she'll think we're crazy. Then, after we find out what she's like, maybe we can tell her the whole thing. But we should find out as much as we can before we say too much ourselves."

"But how will we know whether or not to tell her everything?"

"We'll just have to figure it out," Francine said briskly. "We can use our wonderful telepathy, see if it's really good for anything," she added, and pressed the button.

In a fraction of a second, the inner door buzzed gratingly, and Francine barely had time to push it open before the buzzing stopped. "Sounds like she was standing right by the door, waiting," Francine whispered over her shoulder as they started up the stairs.

"Which floor is it?" Paul asked, looking apprehensively up at the next landing.

"The third," said Francine. "Now remember to try to act normal."

"What?" Paul said, suddenly angry. "What do you mean by—"

"Is that . . . Francine Gill?" came a voice from above them, echoing slightly in the dimly lit stairwell. It was a husky voice.

"Yes," Francine called back. "Mrs. Jaleela?"

Paul looked up again, and saw a woman peering over the railing. "Is that your friend with you? There's nobody else with you?" Mrs. Jaleela inquired, and coughed gently.

"No. Just me and Paul," said Francine, continuing

slowly up the last flight of stairs that led directly to Mrs. Jaleela's landing. From below, Paul saw a tall thin woman with short dark hair step back toward an open doorway as Francine reached the landing. Francine hesitated, then marched toward her. Mrs. Jaleela was wearing a long white robe with a red sash around the waist, and as Francine approached her, she leaned forward and took Francine's hand. She looked quickly at Paul, then back to Francine.

"You are Francine Gill?" said Mrs. Jaleela.

"Yes. Pleased to meet you," said Francine, looking up at Mrs. Jaleela's face, her hand limp in the woman's grasp. Paul had reached the landing, and approached them cautiously.

Mrs. Jaleela's face was narrow and dark, her lips thin and exotically sculpted. Her eyes slipped nervously between Paul and Francine; she smiled briefly and said, "When did you call me up?"

"When did I?" said Francine, sounding baffled.

"I just want to know what day you called me up!" said Mrs. Jaleela.

"It was yesterday, I guess," said Francine. "Tuesday."

"Yes," said Mrs. Jaleela thoughtfully. "And you go to . . . what school?"

"The Wiley School," Francine said rather brusquely, and turned back to Paul. "This is my friend, Paul Rhodes. We're doing the project together."

Paul moved forward and nodded uncomfortably. Mrs. Jaleela peered down into the stairwell, then ushered them into her apartment. She led them through an entry hall and into a twilit living room to a nubbly brown couch. In front of the couch was a coffee table with a vase of red flowers on it.

Mrs. Jaleela sat down across from them in a large white chair. She reached over to a small table beside the chair—which was barely large enough to hold an overflowing ashtray, a pack of cigarettes, and a tall glass with ice in it—took a cigarette and lit it. She leaned toward them. Then she got up and closed the door, sat down, and leaned toward them again. She smiled slightly, but did not say anything.

Paul looked at Francine, who was looking at him. A brief battle went on inside their heads, which Paul won. Then Francine turned reluctantly back to Mrs. Jaleela and said, "You saw that UFO?"

"Yes," said Mrs. Jaleela, leaning back as smoke streamed out of her nose. "Or at least I think I saw it."

"Was it . . . It wasn't hard to see, was it?" said Paul.

"No," said Mrs. Jaleela, slowly bringing her cigarette away from her mouth. "It was quite vivid. I was trying to go to sleep, I remember, in an ugly little room at the motel." Though her body was still languid, she began to speak a little more quickly, and her large dark eyes regarded them with intensity. "At first, it was almost as though I felt something more than I saw it—a change in the atmosphere. I got out of bed and went to the window, and there was a very . . . unusual light in the field behind the motel. By that time Rose was scratching at the screen door, as though she wanted to go out.

And I went to the door and opened it and then stepped out with her." She paused, her eyes floating around the room, and Paul watched a long column of ash drop off her cigarette onto the rug.

"Then what happened?" Francine asked, looking down at the ash on the rug and then back to Mrs. Jaleela.

"Rose was my dog," said Jaleela, as though she hadn't heard Francine. "We were both . . ." She paused to put out her cigarette.

"You were both what?" said Paul and Francine together.

Mrs. Jaleela sighed.

"Well, Rose and I were both pregnant at the time. So Rose was not her usual adventurous self. But when we went outside, I saw that the strange light was actually an object. It was just . . . floating there over the center of the field. So strange . . . so strange. . . ." She stared off at nothing for a moment, then lit another cigarette. "Ordinarily Rose would have been chasing after it and I would have stayed away, I suppose. But somehow I was drawn to it, and Rose was very hesitant. So I started walking toward it, and Rose followed just behind me, growling a little. And then, when I was about fifteen feet away—"

There was a slight creaking noise from another room, as though someone had jumped out of bed. Paul and Francine hardly noticed it, but Mrs. Jaleela seemed startled. She looked toward the living room door, which was closed, then nervously at them, then back to the door.

"And then?" Paul asked her. "You were about fifteen feet away and something happened?"

"Oh," said Mrs. Jaleela. "Yes. We were about fifteen feet away, and then . . . the object seemed to change. It didn't look any different, really; it just *felt* different. It's difficult to explain. You must both think I'm . . ."

"Oh, no, Mrs. Jaleela," Francine insisted. "Please go on."

"Well . . ." Mrs. Jaleela went on slowly. "I believe there was also a change in the sound it was making. You see, it was making a sort of humming sound, and then when we were about fifteen feet away, the change happened. The sound began rising and falling in a very high-pitched whine. And then I felt a very odd sensation, a strange tingling feeling all over, like a minor electric shock, that seemed strongest in my head, and—"

There was another sound from the other room, like a patter of footsteps. Mrs. Jaleela's head spun toward the door. "Oh, dear," she murmured. "I so much hoped . . ." Her voice faded away.

"What's wrong?" Francine asked her.

"Oh, nothing, nothing." She put her cigarette out quickly. "Where was I?"

"The tingling sensation," Paul prompted her.

"Oh, yes." Now she spoke rapidly. "And Rose must have felt it too, because she bared her teeth and snarled, which she very rarely did. I was suddenly quite frightened, but I couldn't run very fast because I was pregnant, but we both went as fast as we could back to the motel, and locked the door and pulled down the shades and called the police. But by the time they got there it was gone. I couldn't sleep all that night, I still felt very strange, and the next day I checked out of the motel as early as—"

At that moment, the vase on the table in front of Paul and Francine began to shiver. Mrs. Jaleela's voice froze in her throat. Her eyes riveted on the vase, and an expression of horror appeared on her face. The vase continued to shiver, and a few drops of water splashed out onto the tabletop. Then, as they watched, two red flowers rose up out of the vase, floated over to Paul and Francine, and dropped gently into their laps.

Dumbfounded, Paul and Francine stared at the flowers, then turned to each other. Mrs. Jaleela covered her face with her hands and shook her head back and forth. The living room door opened and a little boy appeared. He had thick black hair which hung almost to the shoulders of his white pajamas. His face was narrow, with a small straight nose, and when he smiled at Paul and Francine, his shining black eyes seemed to close in slits.

Mrs. Jaleela took her hands away from her face and smiled apologetically at Paul and Francine. "I'm sorry I act so funny sometimes," she said, looking down into her lap and then back at them. "I've been ill recently."

"But—" said Paul, then glanced over at Francine. They silently checked with one another and both agreed that the flowers really had moved. But Mrs. Jaleela seemed to think that she herself had imagined

it. "But we saw it too!" Paul and Francine said at the same moment.

"You're very sweet children," Mrs. Jaleela said sadly, "but please don't try to humor me. It won't work." She reached for another cigarette, and saw the little boy standing in the doorway. "Noah," she said. "Oh, Noah! I wanted you to stay in your room."

The little boy didn't seem to have heard her. He continued to stand there, still grinning at Paul and Francine.

"Is he your son?" Francine asked Mrs. Jaleela.

Mrs. Jaleela nodded, a faint smile on her lips.

"How . . . how old is he?" Paul said.

"Four."

Noah still stood there, smiling at them, motionless. There was something very odd and unchildlike about this behavior that made Paul uncomfortable.

"Hello, Noah," Francine said hesitantly. "How are you today?"

Noah smiled at her, but did not move.

"I'm afraid he can't hear you, dear," Mrs. Jaleela said, lighting the cigarette. "He doesn't hear or speak." And she watched him with her faint ironic smile.

"But why?" said Francine, turning to Mrs. Jaleela with a worried expression. "What's wrong with him?"

"No one seems to know." She shrugged vaguely. "They can't find anything physically wrong. Yet he simply does not respond to noises, and has never spoken a word in his life."

At that moment the conversation was interrupted by

an intense and startling sensation. There was a flash of red in Paul's brain, a feeling of surging excitement, and a mental image of a large black animal hurrying toward him. When it was over, he was looking at Noah. Noah was laughing. In the distance Paul heard a noise, which part of him knew was the buzzer on the front door downstairs. He heard quick footsteps on the stairs. The apartment door swung open, and a large black dog loped into the apartment and into Noah's arms.

Mrs. Jaleela passed her hand over her forehead. She coughed and said, "They're very close. Noah just always seems to know when Cookie's coming back."

"But—" Paul was still reeling from that bright, colorful explosion in his brain. Francine too seemed dazed; he knew she had experienced it just as he had. But what had Mrs. Jaleela experienced? "Do you feel all right?" Paul asked her.

"Oh, it's just these headaches I get sometimes," she said, passing her hand over her forehead again.

And then Cookie was upon them. Big and glossy and black, she put her front legs up on the couch and passionately licked their faces with her long tongue. Relief and gratitude flowed over them, and another intense mental image, this one of Noah running across a field. The image was a familiar one, and all the more so because, like the dream, it was a black and white image.

"Cookie!" Mrs. Jaleela ordered without much conviction. "Cookie! Get down! Leave them alone!"

"Oh, it's all right," gasped Francine, allowing her cheek to be nuzzled while Paul struggled to get his face out of the way. "This isn't . . . Rose?" she managed to add.

"It's Roses's daughter," said Mrs. Jaleela. "Cookie, darling, please leave them alone. She's a Newfoundland, you see, a famous kind of rescue dog, and she likes people."

After one last wet kiss, Cookie jumped down, almost knocking over the vase of flowers, and trotted over to Noah. She proceeded to bathe his face with her large tongue, and Noah chortled happily and hugged her again.

"Whew!" said Paul. "Um . . . Mrs. Jaleela, was Rose pregnant with Cookie when you saw the UFO?"

"Yes," Mrs. Jaleela said softly. "Noah and Cookie are almost exactly the same age, in fact."

"I hope you don't mind me asking you this," Francine said, brushing herself off. "We just keep asking you all these questions. But I was wondering—"

"Oh, it's all right, dear," said Mrs. Jaleela, vaguely waving a freshly lit cigarette at her. "I trust you."

"Well, that's sort of what I was wondering about," Francine went on. "It seemed like you were . . . like you didn't want us to see Noah or know about him; that you were hoping he would stay in his room while we were here."

"Oh," said Mrs. Jaleela. She took a long drag of her cigarette and let the smoke drift slowly out of her nose. "Well, it's just that I've been rather worried lately. Someone has phoned me several times—a man—asking about him. And I've had the peculiar sensation of being followed sometimes, when I'm outside with him." She coughed. "Oh, it's probably all just my imagination." She gestured with her cigarette. "I do seem to be imagining things a lot lately. Still, I really think I have noticed two men behind us quite often. It's probably silly of me, but I do feel threatened somehow," she confessed, sounding slightly embarrassed. "I just want to be sure Noah is safe," she added vehemently. "He's so helpless. That's why I was so hesitant about seeing you, and why I wanted to keep Noah out of the whole thing, if possible."

Paul and Francine did not even have to look at each other now for the dialogue in their heads to take place. Though their thoughts were not exactly in words, the messages were a little clearer than they had been before, perhaps because the need was greater.

It must be the same two men, from Paul. *You must have been right about them following us* (grudgingly). *Let's tell her.*

Wait. Think about it. It will frighten her even more.

But we can explain about being at the Stardust that night. About the telepathy. We can tell her that we're here to help her and Noah.

But she doesn't want to believe in telepathy. I don't think she can. And about the flowers. She saw them move but—

Psychokinesis.

Whatever it was, she couldn't even believe her own eyes. She'll just think we're humoring her. She'll only trust us if she thinks we're just normal everyday kids.

64

But she must have some kind of telepathy too. If we tell her, she can help us.

But we have to be able to do it on our own. If we—

They were interrupted by another blast. This one was in searing, vibrant yellow. It was accompanied by no visual image, only color, and constituted nothing more than a bright greeting, a "Here I am! Can I play too?" feeling.

"Oh, dear." Mrs. Jaleela sighed and bent her head, stroking her forehead again. She looked up at them with her large eyes. "I'm sorry, children, but . . . I'm afraid I'm getting another headache." She smiled faintly. "Did you find out everything you need to know?"

"Um . . . well, I guess so," said Paul.

"Yes, we'll have a good report," said Francine. She stood up. "But, well, we'd love to come back sometime, Mrs. Jaleela. Could we call you up and come over again sometime soon? You're so interesting to talk to. And Noah and Cookie . . ." She turned toward them.

"They do both seem to like you," said Mrs. Jaleela, looking at them too. Cookie trotted over to Francine and rubbed her head against her leg, almost as though she understood what they were saying, and Noah was beaming at them again. "I've never seen either of them respond to strangers so strongly," Mrs. Jaleela continued. "You do seem to make Noah happy. Of course you can come again." She stood up.

"Well, thank you very much," Paul said, as they walked to the door.

65

"See you soon, I hope," said Francine. "Good-bye, Noah; good-bye, Cookie."

Cookie barked sharply and wagged her tail. Noah's smile grew so wide that it seemed as though his small face would not be able to contain it.

Mrs. Jaleela looked at him and smiled. "Good-bye, children," she said, and gently closed the door.

This time the two men were in a car parked across the street and several houses down the block from Mrs. Jaleela's apartment. Now, however, Paul and Francine were keenly aware of their presence.

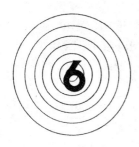

They hurried away from the house, frequently looking behind; but the two men seemed inclined to stay where they were. "I wonder who they *are*," said Paul.

"I'm not sure," said Francine, "but I don't like them one bit. They're not on our side, that's for sure."

"How can you tell?"

"Because if they were, why would they have to be so secretive all the time?"

"They must be interested in Noah," said Paul. "Francine! Those flowers! I can still hardly believe it!"

"I know," Francine murmured. "What was that thing you called it?"

"Psychokinesis. It means being able to make things move just by thinking about it."

"Noah . . ." she murmured. "He has more than just telepathy."

"It's just so hard to believe," said Paul. "But . . . I *saw* it, we *both* saw it. I guess we have to believe it! And the buzzer! He must have rung the buzzer to let Cookie in, just by thinking about it."

"And when he does telepathy, you sure can feel it," Francine said, shaking her head. "It's so strong it almost hurts. Much stronger than what you and I can do. I wonder why?"

"Probably because he was *in utero* when the UFO came," said Paul, showing off some medical knowledge he had picked up. "You know, in his mother's womb."

"Why would that make any difference?" said Francine, sounding duly impressed.

"Well, because the fetus—the unborn baby—is still being formed, and so it's much more susceptible to things that happen to it. Like if a pregnant lady takes drugs, a lot of times they have an effect on the baby. And I guess it's the same with that telepathic ray or whatever it was. I mean we were seven years old when we got it, so it didn't have such a powerful effect on us. That's probably why Noah got psychokinesis, too. I mean he was just a little unformed blob at the time, so the UFO really did a number on him. I'll bet he was the only unborn baby there, and we were the only kids."

"What about Mrs. Jaleela? She must have as much telepathy as we do. She probably just refuses to recognize it because she can't stand to believe in it."

"Well, I don't know," Paul said slowly. "I read somewhere that people's brains change as they get older. For instance, when kids are really young, it's much easier for them to learn languages. Little kids can learn several languages at once without any trouble. But then when you grow up, the brain changes and it's much harder to learn new things. So maybe the ray had a bigger effect on us than on Mrs. Jaleela."

"Well, but whenever Noah sent a message, she said she had a headache."

"Yes, I know. Probably the UFO had some effect on her, but not as much as it had on us, not enough to make her really telepathic, like we are." He looked behind him again, but the two men were not in evidence. "But it had the most effect of all on Noah," he added.

"And on Cookie," said Francine. "Don't forget about Cookie. She was also in . . . in humoro, or whatever you call it."

"*In utero*," Paul corrected her. "Yes, that's right, Cookie is telepathic too. And you know what I think? It's so amazing! I think that—"

"Cookie is sending us the dream," she interrupted, before he had a chance to say it.

"Yes!" Paul said, too excited to be irritated. "Dogs see in black and white, don't they? And the dream is in black and white, just like the thoughts we got from Cookie today."

"And they looked just the same too, with Noah in the field and everything." She sighed. "I guess Cookie really loves Noah, and is worried about him."

"It seems like they're each other's best and only

friend," said Paul. "They can communicate so well with each other."

"But Noah can't communicate with anyone else," Francine said, so softly that he could barely catch her words. She looked away from him. "It's so sad that he can't hear or speak."

"But he doesn't *need* to," Paul insisted. "Maybe that's why he turned out deaf and dumb. He can hear what people are thinking and speak directly into their minds. It's actually a better way to communicate."

"Oh, you're just so pleased about having it yourself that you can't think straight!" Francine said sharply. "It made Mrs. Jaleela a nervous wreck and turned her little boy into a freak. What *good* did it do them? And now those two men are after them."

"And us too," Paul said, looking behind him again. They were on a busier street now, so it was difficult to tell whether the two men were following them or not. "But I can't figure them out. Why don't they just come out and say what they want?"

"Oh, use your head!" snapped Francine. "Don't you realize? Noah's important, really important. He might be the only person in the whole world who can do those things. If the wrong people got hold of him, they could use him to make a lot of money or . . . or to be a spy or something."

"You mean those two men might be secret agents?" said Paul in an excited whisper. "Wow, it's just like being in the movies."

"Oh, no it's not," Francine said impatiently. "You

don't know anything about it. My father was in the army. There were a lot of things he could never talk about. I still remember how my parents used to fight about it. When those people want something, they'll do anything to get it. They don't care about killing a few people to get a secret weapon or something. That's why they're always so secretive, so nobody will find out about the horrible things they do."

For a short time they walked in silence. Paul's thoughts were accompanied by emotional currents from Francine: images of shadowy, purposeful figures full of menace and without pity. He shivered and forgot about being a daring adventurer. People like that were too tough for them to deal with. For a fleeting instant he even wished that none of this had ever happened.

"I guess you're right," he said in a slightly unsteady voice. "If some group like the CIA got their hands on Noah, they could do anything. They could find out anything they wanted, not just about state secrets and documents but about what people were thinking, regular ordinary people. And if they kept it a secret, and nobody knew, nobody would be able to stop them."

"It's so *horrible!*" said Francine, clenching her fists, sounding as though she were struggling not to burst into tears. "That poor little boy! What if they take him and use him and turn him into some kind of monster?"

"But maybe we're getting too carried away," Paul said in an attempt to be comforting and rational. "We're probably just imagining all this."

"We're not imagining those two men," said Francine.

"But how did they find out?"

"I don't know! What difference does it make? They must know pretty much about it, or else they wouldn't be following Noah *and* us."

"I guess," Paul said slowly, "I guess Cookie must be aware of them. She can probably sense them and how dangerous they are. I mean she has a grown-up dog brain, but Noah's still just a kid. He's probably not as perceptive as she is. And we're the only people she can reach out to, so she has to get us to protect Noah. We're the only ones who can sense her thoughts. That *must* be what the dream is all about."

"Yes, but what are we going to do about it?" Francine said, her voice rising hysterically.

"And the full moon," Paul went on, too involved in what he was saying to be embarrassed by her, "probably means they're planning something at that time. Cookie's trying to tell us to get Noah away from them before then."

"But how?" cried Francine, her muddled and hysterical emotions now surging through Paul's mind. "How are we going to get him away from *anybody*?"

"Shhhh!" said Paul. "People are looking at us." They had reached an intersection he knew, and he pulled her off the main thoroughfare onto a quiet residential street near his home.

"What difference does it make?" Francine said bitterly. "We've already given ourselves away. They know we know. They're watching us and they won't let us get away with anything."

Paul made a feeble effort to withstand the powerful torrent of her hopelessness. Without thinking, he looked up at the sky. And then the hopelessness and fear bit down on him stronger than ever before. "Look," he said. He grabbed her shoulder and pointed up at the sky. "Look over there."

Barely visible in the evening light, low in the east, the white moon floated pale and serene above the trees. Only a narrow lopsided sliver missing from one edge disturbed its perfect roundness.

"It's . . . it's almost full," said Francine in a pained hoarse whisper.

"And tomorrow it will be full," Paul murmured.

They stood and stared at it helplessly, experiencing without pleasure a vivid sharing of emotions that only a few hours earlier would have filled them with magical excitement. Indeed, it appeared that with practice, their gift of communication was becoming sharper and more intense. Unfortunately they were now too terrified to pay much attention to it.

At last Paul tore his eyes away from the moon and made another attempt to organize his thoughts. "Well," he said, "we . . . we're going to have to do something."

"I know," said Francine. "We have to try something, even though it's probably useless."

"Let's go over to my house and sit down and try to figure out some kind of plan," Paul suggested. "It's only about a block away from here."

"What about your mother?" Francine said doubtfully.

Paul checked his watch. "Well, I'm sure she's home from work now. But she'll be fixing dinner and stuff. She'll probably leave us alone for a while at least. And I'm just so sick of walking around."

"Oh, all right," she said. "Let's go."

Francine looked around the house curiously. Through her mind, Paul became aware of the large clean rooms, the bright rich colors of the rugs and pictures and furnishings. He remembered what her street was like, and experienced a clear brief picture of cramped rooms and furniture with sheets on it. It occurred to him that he was lucky to live where he did.

"There's nothing wrong with where I live," Francine said quickly. "My mother just doesn't get any alimony, that's all. You don't have to feel sorry for me."

"But—" said Paul, surprised all over again by their quick interchanges of thought. "I didn't mean . . ." He heard noises coming from the kitchen. "Come on, I have to introduce you to my mother. Then we can go somewhere and talk."

His mother was standing at the stove, putting pieces of chicken into a frying pan. When she turned toward them, Paul said, "Hi, Mom, this is Francine. She's in my class."

His mother smiled slightly and nodded. "Hello, Francine," she said. "You must be the new friend Paul's been spending so much time with lately."

"We're working on a project together," Paul told her. "We wanted to do some more work on it this afternoon, so we're just going to go and talk about it now."

74

"You have no books or papers or notes?" his mother asked.

"We didn't find much at the library today," Francine explained.

"Well, we'll be eating dinner in about an hour," his mother said. "Would you like to stay, Francine?"

"Oh. Thank you. But my mother's probably expecting me."

"Feel free to call her up and ask her, if you'd like to."

"Well, maybe I will," said Francine.

"Come on," Paul said. "We have a lot to get done."

They were almost out of the room when his mother said, "Oh, by the way, Paul. Why were you asking me about Nevada the other day?"

"What?" Paul blushed, looked at Francine quickly, then back to his mother. "Oh, no reason. I was just wondering about it, since I hardly remember being there at all."

"Are you sure?" She furrowed her brow and looked closely at him. "Because it's the oddest coincidence. Someone else just asked me about it this morning."

"Who was it?" Paul said just a bit too quickly.

"Oh, a lawyer called me up at the office today. He wanted to know—excuse us for having this personal conversation, Francine—he wanted to know about the divorce, when I filed, how long I was in Nevada, and so on. It wasn't the lawyer your father had before. He said he was representing your father in some case and needed some information that was missing from the files."

"What did you tell him?" Paul asked apprehensively.

"Well, at first I told him the dates and so on. It seemed like a reasonable enough request. Then . . ." She stepped away from the stove and she leaned back against a counter, folding her arms in front of her. "Well, he began asking me about you and it seemed fishy. How old you were at the time, and if the divorce had had much effect on you; things like that. He even wanted to know where you went to school. Well, I saw no reason why I should answer questions like *that*."

"But what did you tell him?"

"Hardly anything, after that. I just said if your father wanted information he could ask me or you directly. After all, he and I are still in touch. Then he started giving some other explanation, and I just hung up on him. But it was odd that you asked me about it the other day."

"Well," Paul began, feeling frightened, but at the same time relieved at what he was about to do, "The reason I asked you was—"

Don't tell her!

But we need help. I bet she'll know what to do.

She'll think we're crazy. And if she believes us about the men, she'll be scared and she won't let you out of the house and we won't be able to do a thing.

But—

Don't tell her!

"Paul, don't you remember?" Francine said out loud. "Miss Keck was talking about Nevada the other day. I bet that's why you wondered about it."

"Oh," Paul said dully. "That's right. I guess that is why I asked you about it."

"Well, it's very odd," his mother said. "I'm going to call your father tonight and ask him what's going on." She turned back to the sputtering chicken.

Upstairs in his room, Paul said, "Maybe we should call the police."

"And tell them what?" said Francine. "That we're getting messages from a dog?"

"But the two men! You can tell the police if somebody's following you!"

"But we can hardly describe them and they haven't threatened us and we've only seen them a few times. The police will just think we're para . . . whatever it is. Crazy."

"Paranoid." He sighed. "I suppose you're right." He turned his desk chair around to face her and sat down. "But what can we do?"

"Well . . ." She sat down on his bed. "All we can do is . . . try to hang around Noah. All day. Maybe we should even skip school. We'll have to think of some kind of explanation for Mrs. Jaleela. But if we're hanging around, they probably couldn't . . . take him away or anything."

"But what if they . . . take us?"

"Oh, I don't know," said Francine, and bounced irritably on the bed. "We'll just have to see what happens. I'm scared too, you know."

Paul had been idly staring out of the window that was beside the bed. Suddenly he stood up and moved toward it. "Francine!" he whispered.

"What? What's the matter?" she said, looking up at him, unaware of the window behind her.

"Francine!" He was having trouble getting the words out. "Francine. Behind you. Look."

By the time she turned around, the two men had gotten out of the car and were moving quickly toward the front door.

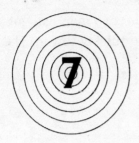

The doorbell rang.

Standing close together in Paul's room, they listened to his mother's quick footsteps across the hall and the rattle and squeak of the door opening.

"Mrs. Rhodes?" The deep male voice floated up faintly from downstairs.

"Yes."

The voices were almost impossible to hear from where they stood. Paul beckoned silently, and he and Francine crept across the upstairs hall to the top of the stairs.

"We'd like to talk to you for a few minutes. May we come in?"

"But who are you? What do you want?" She sounded slightly alarmed.

"We're here on important government business. If you just keep calm, there won't be any trouble."

"Any trouble?" she said, not calm at all. "What do you mean, *trouble*? And how do I know who you are?"

Paul and Francine stood motionless, staring at each other, a mental picture of what was happening downstairs moving back and forth between them. There was a brief pause in the conversation, during which they both imagined the men displaying badges or identification of some sort.

"Oh, I see," Paul's mother said, now sounding suspicious and almost hostile. "But I *don't* see why your agency should have any interest in me, and I still don't see why I should let you in."

"As a matter of fact, it's not you that we're interested in. Is your son home?"

Paul watched Francine chew on her lip. Though he felt immobilized with fear, his mind was working quickly, as was Francine's, both focusing down at Paul's mother the strongest messages of warning they could muster up. His mother, after all, had been at the Stardust too.

"Oh . . ." His mother seemed confused. "Oh . . . N-no, he's not. He hasn't come home from the library yet. What do you want with him?"

"We can explain better inside," the man said. They heard footsteps, the squeak and rattle and thud of the door closing, and the click of the lock.

"But . . ." protested his mother. "But I didn't say you could come in like this. I—"

"Please, Mrs. Rhodes. This is more important than you realize. It's so important that . . . we really can't tell you very much about it. You'll just have to trust us."

"But what do you want with Paul? What has he done?"

"Nothing, yet. But he is in a position to interfere with some very important plans of ours, plans that are of . . . international significance. Highly classified plans. For the good of everyone, as well as for his own safety, we are going to see that he does not interfere."

"What are you talking about? Paul? He's only a little boy! You must be out of your minds!"

"But that isn't all." Now it was the other man speaking. "Your son also has a positive value for us, Mrs. Rhodes. I'm not at liberty to explain exactly why. The fact is that we need him, however, and we are prepared to be very generous."

"You must be joking!" She sounded less frightened now, and rather skeptical.

"We are very serious," the first man said. "We are also, at the moment, pressed for time. When will he be back?"

"Oh, ah . . . he should be back any minute now."

"Well, we only have a few minutes to wait, but while we do, we might as well tell you as much as we can of what this is all about."

Now Paul was sending a different message to his

mother. Francine caught on right away and added her own energy to it. And, amazingly, in a few seconds his mother said, "Well, why don't we . . . why don't we go into my study. We'll be more comfortable there."

"You're sure he'll be back soon? He has no plans for this evening?"

"I'm expecting him and one of his friends for dinner, and we always eat at the same time every day. They should be down . . . uh, here in just a few minutes." The voices faded as they moved toward the rear of the house.

"Oh, may I ask who his friend is? You see . . ." They heard the door to his mother's study click shut, and the voices stopped.

Paul was still watching Francine's face. Even though there was a strong element of "I told you so," in her thoughts, he nevertheless felt more respect and less irritation for her at this moment than ever before. She was brilliant! "You knew," he whispered. "You knew exactly who they were!"

She shrugged. "I . . . I had some experience with that kind of government thing before, because of my father, that's all. Let's get out of here."

"You're really sure that we should—"

She put her finger to her lips, then pointed, indicating that they could talk outside. They made their way down the steps as quietly as possible and then across the front hall. The door, unfortunately, made quite a lot of noise, but since the study door was closed, there was a good chance that the men would hear nothing. And since the study was at the back of the house, there was no way they could see Paul and Francine dash across the front yard and duck behind some thick shrubbery in a neighbor's garden.

"Important plans," Paul said, panting slightly. "That means Noah."

"Yes, and they're going to do it now. We don't have much time."

"But it still isn't a full moon."

"So Cookie was one day off," said Francine. "That's still pretty good for a dog."

"I wonder if they know about Cookie?"

"I don't know. They might not. But thank heavens she's around! They'd already have all of us if it weren't for her. She's done everything. Come on." She started off quickly in the direction of Mrs. Jaleela's apartment.

Paul trotted along beside her. "But, Francine, are you really sure that we should interfere? I mean, it's so dangerous, we could get into so much trouble, it's probably against the law. Maybe . . . maybe what they want to do *isn't* so terrible."

"But Paul, don't you see? They're not giving us any choice. We have this special gift, and Noah has that fantastic power. We have to be able to decide for ourselves how to use it, and so does Noah. But once they get hold of us, it will be too late. *They* will be telling *us* what to do."

Paul was thinking hard. Logically he was beginning to see that, once again, Francine was right. "I guess if they meant to let Noah use his powers in his own way, they wouldn't be afraid of us interfering. I mean, they obviously want to keep the whole thing a secret; *that's* what gives them away. And it shouldn't be a secret. It shouldn't be 'highly classified.' It's a wonderful, important thing that everybody should know about!"

"Now you're catching on," said Francine. With her purposeful expression and her hair blowing back in the gathering evening wind, she looked, suddenly, just the way she did in the dream. "I swear, Paul, for somebody who's so good in school, it sure takes you a while sometimes. I mean, it's just like you said before. Anybody who has control of Noah and keeps it a secret could do *anything*; they'd have such . . . such an incredible amount of power to control other people."

"Yes," said Paul slowly, "and Noah will only be safe if the whole world knows about him."

The sky was purple now, the moon huge and bright and hanging low over the horizon. It was quite dark under the sighing trees, and all at once the streetlights flickered on. Paul was reminded of the menacing, swirling lights in the dream. What could they mean?

"I wonder what your mother was thinking," said Francine. "It was pretty amazing the way she told them you weren't home, and then got them away from the door."

"It sure was," Paul said, feeling proud of his mother, and also, for the first time, feeling something of her equal.

"Do you think it means she has telepathy too?" Francine asked him.

It occurred to Paul then that Francine had been asking him a lot of questions recently, as though she considered him an authority about certain things. Something had changed her attitude toward him; she almost seemed to respect him now. "Well," he said, "she may have received some effect from the ray, but not much. Even less than Mrs. Jaleela. She did get what we were trying to tell her, but I bet it was pretty vague. She probably thought they were her own ideas, and didn't realize they were coming from us."

"Paul," said Francine abruptly, "we have to tell Mrs. Jaleela the truth tonight."

"I thought you said we couldn't tell her."

"Well, now I think we have to, so she'll understand why we have to keep Noah away from those men."

"And then what do we do?"

"You keep asking me that!" Francine cried out, startling him, "I don't know what we're going to do. We'll just have to see what happens."

They approached Mrs. Jaleela's building carefully, avoiding the sidewalks and the streetlights, and sneaking through the darkness behind bushes and under trees. There was no one else on the sidewalk, but there was a car parked across the street from the building, though it was too dark to tell if anyone was inside it. They slid quietly through the front door and pushed Mrs. Jaleela's bell.

They waited, Francine's hand on the doorknob, but the buzzing did not come. "What if they're not here?" Paul whispered. "What if they got them already?"

"Oh, stop—" Francine began.

"Who is it?" Mrs. Jaleela's voice was tinny and crackled with static through the intercom.

"Francine and Paul," Francine said, keeping her voice down in case anyone was listening outside.

"Who is it?" came Mrs. Jaleela's voice again. "I can't hear you."

"Francine and Paul," shouted Francine. "We were just here this afternoon. Please let us in, it's important."

At last the door buzzed; they were through in an instant and clattering up the stairs. Mrs. Jaleela was standing on the landing outside her door. She smiled wanly at them. "Hello, children," she said. "I didn't expect you back so soon."

"We had to, Mrs. Jaleela," said Francine. "It's important. Can we come in?"

"Certainly." Mrs. Jaleela ushered them in to the same seats as before, turned off the television set, and sat down across from them. She picked up a cigarette that was still burning in the ashtray. "What's on your minds?" she said.

"A lot," said Francine. "Is Noah here?"

"I just put him to bed. But why?"

"And Cookie?"

"She always stays with him at night. Francine, dear, what—"

And then Cookie trotted into the room. She made two short, yelping little barks, twisted her head in an odd way, trotted around in a nervous little circle and then barked again. The dream feeling of danger flowed over them, a vivid black and white image of Noah running, and an urgency to act that was stronger than ever before.

"Cookie! Be quiet! What's the matter with you?" Mrs. Jaleela said sharply.

"It's okay, Mrs. Jaleela," said Francine. "You see—I don't know how to tell you this—but Noah's in danger."

"What? In danger?" Mrs. Jaleela leaned forward. "What are you talking about?"

"Didn't you say you felt like you were being followed?" Paul said. "And that someone had called you up and asked about Noah?"

"Yes? Yes? Go on!"

"Well those same men have been following us too, and today they came over to my house and they're probably on their way over here right now."

Mrs. Jaleela stood up. "What do you mean? Who are they?"

"They're government agents, from the CIA or something," said Francine. "They want us, but they want Noah more, because—you *have* to believe this—because he has amazing powers. We do too, a little bit. And they want to take him and keep him secret and *use* him. And we can't let them. And Cookie has it too, and she's been—"

Mrs. Jaleela was fumbling frantically with another cigarette, her hands shaking. "Have you gone insane, little girl?" she said angrily. "What are you trying to do to me? I can't understand you. Special powers?"

"But you've seen it yourself; you've probably been

seeing it for years," said Paul. "Don't you remember this afternoon? Those flowers, they floated right into our laps. Noah did that. I *know* you saw it."

Mrs. Jaleela closed her eyes and shook her head. "But . . . but that isn't real. It's just . . . it's just me, it's just something wrong with me. It doesn't really happen."

"But we saw it *too*, Mrs. Jaleela!" cried Francine. "It's real! You are not crazy! We both saw it."

Mrs. Jaleela ran her hand through her hair in a confused manner. "But . . . but that's impossible."

"No it isn't," said Paul. "And that's not all Noah does. He's telepathic. He can tell what we're thinking, he can probably tell what you're thinking, and he can send his thoughts to us. It's because of that UFO you saw when you were pregnant with him. And we were there too, in that same motel, and it affected us. And those two men want to make him use it for—"

The doorbell rang.

"Don't answer it!" cried Paul and Francine together.

"But this is all . . . nonsense," Mrs. Jaleela murmured, moving slowly into the hall in a kind of daze. "Maybe there is something to what you're saying about Noah, but . . . but I don't understand why you're so upset, why . . . why would those people want to hurt him?" Her hand was poised at the button beside the door.

"Don't answer it!" Francine pleaded.

"But I'm expecting company," said Mrs. Jaleela, sounding angry again. "Don't tell me what to do in my own house. And I'm afraid it's time for you to go." She pressed the button.

They heard the buzzer go off below. Then heavy footsteps running up the stairs. Mrs. Jaleela was clearly surprised. "That doesn't sound like Ethel," she murmured.

"It's not Ethel, it's those men!" said Francine in a furious whisper. "And now they're going to get in."

Cookie growled deep in her throat, and urged them to follow her into Noah's room. "Don't tell them we're here," Francine whispered to the now completely confused Mrs. Jaleela. "And don't tell them Noah's here. Tell them he's out of town, visiting a relative or something. *Please.*"

They left Mrs. Jaleela standing helplessly by the door as the first knock sounded, and ran after Cookie. She led them down a narrow corridor and into a small bedroom. It was dark, but there was enough moonlight coming through the window for them to see Noah sitting up in bed in his white pajamas. Paul closed the bedroom door quietly.

Cookie hurried over to Noah, who hugged her and then looked up at Paul and Francine. He grinned happily and clapped his small hands together with excitement, and then greeted them with a flash of vivid, welcoming orange. A teddy bear bounced twice on the bed beside him, then did a slow somersault in the air and tumbled to the floor at their feet.

"Now what are we going to—" Paul began as the flash died away.

Francine shook her head violently and covered her

mouth with her hand. *Don't talk. Think!* she ordered.

Can you hear what they're saying in the front hall? he asked her.

I'm trying to!

One of the men's voices was the clearest, though it was difficult to tell whether it was the same voice they had heard at Paul's house. ". . . the truth . . . not to be afraid," he seemed to be saying. "We just want . . . very important . . . trust. . . . Don't listen to . . . children . . . hysterical . . . son in danger. . . ."

She's going to give in, I know it, thought Paul.

And they'll be in here in a minute, agreed Francine, her mind in a turmoil.

Cookie broke in on them with a clear, urgent picture of the four of them climbing out of the window.

Paul hurried to the window at the back of the room. There was a narrow iron fire escape outside it, with stairs leading down into blackness. *Let's go,* thought Paul to all of them. He pushed up the window, which protested with a sharp squeak, and Francine gathered up Noah. Cookie flowed out of the window, teetered uncomfortably on the edge of the fire escape landing, then turned back to them. Paul clambered out miserably (he hated high places), but tried not to think about where he was as he followed Francine's order and opened his arms to accept Noah as she passed him through the window. Noah, still unaware of any danger, wriggled happily in his arms, sending sparks of excitement through their heads. *What if I drop him?* Paul worried.

Let me take him.

Francine emerged onto the fire escape, and Paul handed Noah back to her. Then he turned and followed Cookie slowly down the stairs, keeping close to the side of the building. Cookie hated the fire escape as much as he did, slipping occasionally on the metal grating, but she made very little noise. Unfortunately, the fire escape ended abruptly in midair, fifteen feet above the ground.

How stupid! Paul thought angrily.

They do it so people can't break in this way. If there's a fire, you're supposed to jump.

What about Noah?

Cookie turned around, licked Noah's foot with her long tongue, hesitated for a moment, then sailed into the air. She landed quietly, like a cat, then paced below them, her eyes on Noah.

I can't jump while I'm holding him, wailed Francine on the edge.

Then what are we going to do?

There was a noise in the bedroom above, and a striped, irregular patch of light flashed across them. Paul didn't dare look up, but he clearly heard Mrs. Jaleela cry out, "Down there, on the fire escape!"

Grab on to him with me, Paul! We'll both jump together!

But—

Don't think about it, just do it!

Paul put one arm around Francine and the other firmly around Noah. *One, two, three, Go!* counted Francine. They each took a deep breath, and jumped.

Their landing was surprisingly, even miraculously, gentle after a fall from that height; they both landed on their feet. But they did not pause to wonder about it. There were footsteps on the fire escape now, and Cookie was urging them on again, looking back at them as she hurried into the shadows behind the building. Obviously, she knew the best way to get away from the building without being seen. Francine tightened her grip on Noah, who still seemed to think the whole thing was a marvelous game; and without looking back, they stumbled after Cookie into the darkness.

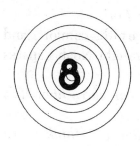

8

At the back of the building was a ramshackle garage, and behind it, a dark, narrow alley. There were no lights here and Cookie, being black, was difficult to see. But her thoughts reached out like a bright beacon, leading them quickly and quietly down the alley, around a corner into another long alley, and then out onto an unfamiliar street.

I wonder where she's taking us? thought Paul.

I guess it doesn't matter, as long as we get away from them.

The sparks coming from Noah suddenly erupted into a purple shower of longing and confusion. *I want Mommy! Where is Mommy? Where is she? I want her I want her.* And he squirmed in Francine's arms.

It's all right, Noah. We'll see her in a minute. Isn't this fun?

Fun, Noah, we're having fun fun fun!

And, from Cookie, a wave of warmth, comfort, and protection that, after a moment, brought Noah's sparks of excitement back again.

I don't know how much longer I can carry him. He's getting pretty heavy.

Well, maybe you can put him down. I think we've lost them. It's lucky his pajamas have feet.

They were on a busier street now, and Cookie was not moving quite so fast. Francine set Noah down on the sidewalk, and they each took one of his hands. Cookie turned back for a moment to lick his face; Noah chortled and splashed them all with affection and glee.

Good thing he's not moody, thought Francine.

There were cheap restaurants and bars with bright neon lights around them now. Gritty dust blew along the sidewalk, and a man weaving down the street almost bumped into Francine. Cookie loped along only a foot in front of them, moving slowly, no longer sure of where she was going.

"She's not being the leader anymore," Paul said aloud, not wanting to offend her.

"We'll just have to decide where to go ourselves," said Francine. "We can't depend on her for everything."

Suddenly Cookie stiffened, spun around and barked loudly. A large dark car pulled over to the curb just a few yards behind them. There were two men in the front seat, and in the back was Mrs. Jaleela. She leaned out of the window and shouted something at them, but they did not stop to listen.

Hide and go seek, Noah! Shrieked Francine against Noah's intense yellow blast of recognition and desire to go back to his mother. *It's a game! She has to try to find us. This time* you *take him, Paul.*

Paul scooped him up. *But where?*

No answer came from Cookie. Her head darted around frantically, but now there was no familiar alley to be found.

This way! commanded Francine. She dashed ahead, then plunged down a flight of steps into a subway station.

The subway, Noah. The subway is fun! Did you ever go on the subway before? Paul thought desperately at him. Noah turned his head, disturbed, as Paul struggled down the steps with him. But when he saw that Cookie was still with them he relaxed again.

Francine was already at the turnstile, hopping nervously. "I don't have any money, Paul."

"But I don't know if I have any either!" He set Noah down and fumbled through his pockets. His hand emerged at last with some change. "Here, Francine, this is for you and this is for me and I don't think we have to pay for the other two."

"But where are they?"

Paul turned back to where he had set Noah down, but there was no sign of him or of Cookie. "But he was just there one second ago!"

"Maybe he went back up the steps to his mother!"

"Oh, *no!*" Paul moaned, and started back for the steps.

"Wait! There they are, on the platform!" cried Francine.

Noah and Cookie, both looking around with wonder at the filthy subway station and the crowds of people, were standing on the other side of the turnstiles, dangerously close to the track. As Noah peered over the edge, the shriek and rumble of an approaching train came echoing down the tunnel.

"But how did they get over there?" said Paul as he dropped his money into the slot and pushed through.

"*I* don't know. Just get hold of him before the train comes."

Paul dashed across the platform, grabbed Noah, and pulled him away from the track as the train screamed into the station. Noah jumped up and down and clapped his hands, sending out exploding sparks more intense than the high-pitched squeal of the brakes.

"If he doesn't get that under control, it's going to drive me crazy," Paul complained as he picked up Noah and stepped onto the train.

"Well, maybe sometime we can try to teach him to tone it down, if we ever get out of this mess." *Come on, Cookie.* Francine stood in the doorway of the train and beckoned to the dog. Cookie peered into the train, then drew her head back, then peered into the train again. *Come on, Cookie, it's safe, it's okay, you won't get hurt. Do it for Noah. . . . Oh, no!*

"What is it?" Paul said aloud. He turned away from Noah, still grasping his hand firmly, and looked toward the stairway. The two men had reached the bottom, and Mrs. Jaleela was right behind them.

Cookie saw them too, and bounded, at last, onto the train. But the train did not seemed inclined to move. They watched helplessly through the train windows as the two men and Mrs. Jaleela dropped coins into the slots, pushed through the turnstiles, and hurried toward them.

Where can we go? What can we do?

I don't know! You think of something!

Mommy, Mommy, here I am, here I am! You found us!

But as the two men barreled toward the train, the doors of their car slammed shut. The men paused for an instant, then ran down the platform searching for a car that was still open. Mrs. Jaleela looked in at them briefly, furiously shaking her head, then turned and ran after the men, disappearing from view. A moment later the train groaned, jerked forward, and rumbled into the tunnel.

"Did they get on?" asked Paul, peering anxiously toward the back of the car.

"Not on this car, but they still might be on the train."

Noah looked up at Paul and smiled. *This is fun, but why didn't Mommy come?*

You'll see her pretty soon, Francine told him. *Isn't it fun being on this train, and being with us?*

Oh, wonderful being with you! There was a flood of

orange, with ecstatic blue spirals dancing and sizzling across it. *You understand me like Cookie, not as loud as Cookie, but better, more like me. You're the only ones. It's wonderful! Only . . . why are you afraid? I don't like to be afraid. Why didn't Mommy come?*

Lights flashed past them as the train careened through the dark tunnel. Swaying, Paul and Francine turned to look at each other over Noah's head. "I don't know what to tell him," Francine said aloud.

"I'm sure getting tired of only thinking about how much *fun* this is all the time," said Paul. "Why shouldn't we tell him the truth?"

"It's just that if he's scared, he'll be harder to handle. We have to keep him amused." *Noah,* she thought, *can you hear other people besides me and Paul and Cookie?*

I listen to Mommy a lot. She can't hear me when I try to talk to her.

How about other people? asked Paul. *Like on this train?*

So much on this train! All different, confusing, hard to understand.

What about that man, right there? asked Francine, indicating a fat man reading a newspaper.

Ummmm. There was a brief pause. *Well, on top it's kind of:* "The two men were wearing heavy overcoats and woolen skiers' masks over their faces. 'They must have been dying of the heat,' commented Miss Basket, the teller. Nevertheless, they remained cool as they left the bank with ten thousand dollars in ten- and twenty-dollar bills." *Then underneath that it's about riding on*

this train and hating it and wishing he was in a big car with a driver and how they shouldn't let dogs on the train. He doesn't like Cookie. He wants to kick her!
There was a red splash of anger. Suddenly the man's newspaper tore itself out of his hands, hovered in front of him for an instant, and then wrapped itself around his head.

Noah! You shouldn't have done that!
But he wanted to kick Cookie!
For a moment the man just stood there waving his hands helplessly in front of him. Then he peeled the newspaper off his face and swung around angrily.

"Wha . . . ? Who did that?" he demanded.

A few people in the car turned to look at him, seeming apprehensive and yet bored, except for one old lady who had witnessed the whole event. "That's what they all say," she observed in a high-pitched quavering wail. "They always say that! Leave them alone, just leave them alone, I'm sick of all of them. Just leave them alone, if you ask me!"

"It would be interesting to find out what's going on inside *her* head," Paul murmured to Francine, turning sideways to lean closer to her. His eye caught a flurry of movement at the back of the car and he peered closer, then grabbed Francine's shoulder. "There they are!" he whispered. "They've been coming through the cars and now they're on this one!"

Francine looked quickly, then spun around. "We have to get into the next car!" she said.

"With Noah and Cookie? How can we?"

"Paul, we can't let them catch us!"

But just at that moment the brakes squealed, the train jerked several times, almost knocking them down, then slid into a brightly lit station and stopped. *Off the train, fast!* ordered Francine. They pushed through bodies, dragging Noah along with them; Cookie squirmed in between legs, and they surged from the train locked in a tight knot of people.

"I wonder where we are," said Francine as they hurried across the platform, looking for the exit.

"Wonderland," Paul read. "That's the name of this stop. Wonderland. How weird."

"Wonderland!" repeated Francine. "So that's where we are. Come on, there's the steps. Are they behind us?"

"It's hard to tell, there's so many people."

Where are we going?

Come on, Noah, up the steps.

But where are we going?

Wonderland, Noah. We're going to Wonderland.

But what's Wonderland?

It's a surprise. You'll find out in just a minute.

At the top of the steps they found themselves on the edge of a large, windy parking lot. On the other side of the parking lot, the word *Wonderland* flashed in bright red neon against the sky. Colored lights whirled behind it, and they could hear faint tinny music and distant shrieks.

"It's an amusement park!" Paul groaned.

"Of course," said Francine. "The perfect place to lose them. Come on."

"But," said Paul, hurrying along beside her rather reluctantly, "but I hate amusement parks."

"So what?" she said irritably. "It will be easy to get lost in it, there'll be crowds of people, and it will keep Noah happy. And anyway, I happen to love amusement parks."

Paul sighed and looked behind. There was a streetlight beside the subway exit, which was getting farther and farther behind them now. Had the two men already come out, or were they still down in the station, or even on the train?

"Paul!"

He turned back and saw the lights of a slowly moving car one foot in front of him. He darted to the side, barely missing it.

"Look where you're going!"

"But I was just . . ." For one brief second he looked behind again. And in that second he clearly saw the two men and Mrs. Jaleela under the streetlight. One of them pointed toward the parking lot, and they started to run.

"I saw them!" he said. "They're still following us. They're in the parking lot now!"

"We've just got to get into that park! Carry Noah; he can't go fast enough."

But why are we running away? Noah demanded as Paul clumsily pulled him off the pavement, settled him into his arms, and kept on running.

We're just in a hurry to get there, Francine lamely explained. *Noah, it's so much fun there! They have good things to eat, and cotton candy, and all sorts of games to play, and rides, wonderful rides to go on.*

The Wonderland sign curved across the top of a large, ornate iron gateway, the entrance to the park. As Paul ran through it, Noah turned and squirmed in his arms. *Wait for Cookie! I want Cookie to come too!*

They had almost forgotten about Cookie. She stood just outside the gateway, her tongue hanging out, shrinking back from the crowds and noise on the other side. Her dream feeling of fear washed over them again, stronger now than it had ever been.

They hurried back to the dog, and Francine kneeled beside her. *Don't be afraid, Cookie, it's just a place where people have fun. No one will hurt you. It's the best way to keep Noah safe.*

Cookie whined deep in her throat, and the dream feeling flowed over them again.

Paul was still holding Noah. "Maybe she knows something we don't know," he suggested, frightened now by the memory of the dream as well as by the pursuing men.

"But what could she know?" asked Francine. "It doesn't make sense. She's just afraid because she's never been to a place like this before." She stroked Cookie's back soothingly. *Please, Cookie. Everything will be okay. We've just got to get lost inside here or else they'll catch us. It's the only thing we can do now.*

Cookie growled, then turned to look toward the parking lot.

"There they are!" cried Francine, pointing. "Come on, Cookie!"

Cookie turned toward them again and took a few slow

104

steps forward. A sort of spasm passed over her as she moved through the gateway. Then she looked up questioningly at Francine.

"Over there!" Francine directed. "It's crowded and we have to get away from this entrance."

Now there was noise all around them—the ringing of bells in game booths, music blaring and throbbing and tinkling, the grinding of machinery and the clacketing of wheels. Behind it all rose the shrieks of people plunging and spinning through the air. Red, blue, and yellow lights whirled against the dark sky; lacy chains of white glittered and looped across the buildings. Fading paint peeled from the wooden booths, and brightly colored trash danced and fluttered past their feet as they hurried through the crowd.

Noah squirmed continuously in Paul's arms, his dazzled eyes moving rapidly from one amazing sight to the next. His bleeps and sparks and crackles of wonder and excitement flashed through their heads, not quite blotting out the tense and foreboding images from Cookie.

They paused beside a large carousel that glittered with many mirrors and garlands of light. Wheezing and puffing with effort, it emitted a blaring, tuneless waltz as the stiff wooden horses rose and dipped and children screamed ecstatically. Noah leaned forward, almost tumbling out of Paul's arms. *I want to go on that thing I want to ride on that I want to get on let me get on!*

"Should we take him on it?" Paul asked Francine.

"Not yet." She peered anxiously into the crowd behind them. "It's too soon. I'm not sure we've lost them yet."

105

They moved on, and Noah was immediately distracted by other sights. All around them were people of all ages, getting in their way and bumping into them. And perhaps it was because there were so many different kinds of people everywhere that Paul and Francine, though they were doing their best to be alert, did not notice the ones they were looking out for until it was too late.

The only warning was a sharp bark from Cookie and a sudden flash of panic from Francine. Paul turned to see one of the men holding a struggling Francine firmly by the elbow. His eyes raced across the crowd and spotted the other man and then Mrs. Jaleela, coming at him from different directions. Both escape routes were cut off, and he stood frozen, unable to think.

Run, Paul! Francine screamed silently at him. *Don't just stand there! Get away from them!*

But where? he screamed back at her. *They're on both sides now!*

Over there! To the left! The Ferris wheel! Get on it! They can't get you there!

Paul did not think; he ran. For so long now, his only object had been to keep Noah away from the men, that no other consideration crossed his mind. He sprinted past Francine, avoided the man who was holding her, and dashed up the rickety wooden steps at the base of the giant wheel. He did not listen to Cookie's howl or Mrs. Jaleela's screams as he dropped some coins into the operator's outstretched palm and allowed himself to be helped, with Noah, into the swinging wooden seat.

He did not think as the safety bar clicked into place in front of them. The operator stepped to the side and pulled the lever, and with a heavy groaning sigh the machinery came to life.

It was not, in fact, until he was swept backwards with a sudden swift rush high, high into the air that he remembered how much he hated Ferris wheels, and realized the significance of those menacing lights, swinging in arcs, in the dream.

For a moment, but only a moment, Noah was startled by the unexpected sensation. But as they sailed up over the top of the wheel, where all the lights of the carnival were spread out below them, plummeted down toward the ground and swooped up again, Noah erupted with swirling cascades of joy and delight.

With his left hand Paul gripped the safety bar. With his right arm he hugged Noah's small body tightly against himself. His eyes were squeezed shut, his teeth clenched, his stomach tightened. He tried not to think about the fact that their only protection was the thin wooden bar, tried to forget that his legs and feet were just dangling out into empty space.

Oh, wonderful, wonderful, wonderful! sang out Noah. *Oh, the feeling! We see everything, everywhere. All the people. Mommy! Hi Mommy, hi down below! Can you see me?* And Paul felt the seat swing wildly back and forth as Noah leaned forward to wave.

Stop it Noah! Sit back! Don't make it swing, don't move!

But why you afraid? This is wonderful, wonderful! Don't be afraid. Please have fun with me. I want you to have fun.

Why *am* I afraid? Paul asked himself as another burst of delirious, infectious joy blossomed in his head. Noah's emotions were difficult to ignore. Cautiously, he opened his eyes. They were flying over a gorgeous sea of lights; and as they dipped down closer, the sea of lights became a sea of faces staring up at them with fascination. And then up again, and again the world was a delicate web of many colors, and they were free in the wind.

His hand unclenched a bit on the safety bar, his shoulders relaxed, and he turned his head to the side to see more. *Now you feel better!* crowed Noah. *See how nice? See how fun and nice?*

Now that Paul was high over the park, he could see even more clearly how the lights below and the lights on the Ferris wheel, itself, resembled the swinging lights in the dream. But that doesn't make sense, argued the part of him that was now beginning to enjoy the ride. Cookie couldn't know we were going to come here; she couldn't know we were going to go on the Ferris wheel. Nobody was thinking about it, so she couldn't have sensed it. Those lights in the dream must be just a coincidence; she couldn't have been warning us against coming here.

And he relaxed a little more, and gave in to Noah's penetrating waves of joy and the intoxication of the ride. As they plummeted down again, he could see that his own group was standing in front of the crowd. Cookie was the closest to the wheel, and just behind her was Francine, the man still gripping her elbow. They all stood without moving, their eyes riveted on Noah and Paul. Francine's thoughts grew stronger as he swooped closer to them, agonized thoughts of fear and hopelessness. *Everything will be all right,* he tried to broadcast to her. *We can just stay on this all night; they'll never catch us now!*

But all at once the great wheel slowed, creaking, until they were drifting, not soaring. When it finally stopped with a jerk that sent their seat swinging back and forth, they were near the bottom. The operator swung open the safety bar of the seat just below them and the people climbed out. Then, to Paul's relief, he moved the wheel so that their seat swung one notch higher up, away from the loading platform. They were the last ones on; they would be the last ones to get off. He was still reeling from Noah's emotions and the pleasure of the ride, but the practical part of him knew that this delay would give him time to decide what to do next.

Do you want to go on again, Noah? he asked, reaching into his pocket.

Noah nodded vehemently and bounced up and down

on the seat. *Yes yes yes again let's go again.* The seat swung wildly as they moved up another notch. Now they were halfway to the top.

Paul reached out for Francine. *We're going again,* he thought as loudly as he could. *I have enough money for one more ride. It's the only thing I can think of to do.*

Don't go on it again. Her mood was bleak, and the message came through more feebly than usual. *Cookie's real worried. And it won't do any good. They'll just grab you as soon as you get off. This creep has a grip like iron.*

The seat moved up another notch. *Oh, don't be depressed,* he told her. *I feel good for some reason. I think it's going to be okay. I know I'll think of something. If we go on again, maybe we can sneak off it somehow when they're not looking, and get away.*

He peered down at her through the maze of lights and spokes. It was difficult to see her expression, but she was shaking her head back and forth at him. . . . *Can hardly hear you* . . . came the faint message. It seemed, however, that she was more worried than she had been just a moment before. . . . *to Cookie . . . listen to her. . . . not again . . . better get off. . . . worried, really worried.*

The car moved up another notch. They were almost at the top now. He had been trying to ignore Cookie's unpleasant images, but now he opened his mind to them again. They were a good deal stronger than Francine's, and hit out at him with all the terror of the dream.

112

But the terror was vague. She didn't seem to know exactly what she was afraid of; she just wanted Noah off the Ferris wheel. Far below, mingled with the music and the screams and the babble of voices, he heard her bark frantically. *But if we get off now, they'll just catch us,* he projected with all the strength he had. *She doesn't know anything about it. She's just afraid because she thinks it's dangerous.*

I can hardly . . . too far. . . . Just get off. . . . Don't be stupid. . . . The seat moved up another notch. They were now at the very top.

Cookie worries a lot. Noah's message was shatteringly clear compared to the others. He grinned at Paul, swinging his legs back and forth and causing their seat to sway—and to creak ominously. It occurred to Paul that it hadn't creaked like that before. But Noah was still talking to him and it was impossible to concentrate on anything else. *Cookie is always afraid something will happen to me. She doesn't know how much fun this is. A lot of stuff she doesn't understand. I want to go again!* And to emphasize how much he meant it, he gave an extra powerful kick with his legs.

Then it happened. Paul heard the squeak of metal and a sharp *ping* as something bounced past him. There was a sickening lurch, and Noah fell heavily against him as the seat gave way. *No no no!* The unbearable feeling of falling, of nothing beneath him, and a grinding crack and a terrible hoarse scream and black black blinding panic.

He stopped screaming and opened his eyes. He was

still up in the air, and Noah was still clinging to him. And the seat was still there underneath them, but the seat was different now. With panic ringing and burning through every muscle of his body, Paul twisted his head slightly and looked up. One end of the seat, above him now, was still attached to the wheel by its vertical metal bar. But on the other side, the vertical bar had given way.

By some miracle the edge of the seat had come to rest on one of the horizontal crossbeams that held the two huge discs of the wheel together, so that now the seat hung at a forty-five-degree angle. He was sitting on the bottom end, partly on the back of the seat and partly on the armrest. Noah was weighing down on him; Paul was hugging him with one arm, and with the other he was clutching desperately at the beam that supported them.

He was aware now of the crowd screaming below. He moved his head slightly to look down, and the seat teetered precariously. *What happened, what happened? Why are we like this? Don't let go, don't let go!* Noah's panic boiled and bubbled inside him, but it was no worse than his own.

He froze, gripping the beam more tightly, and the seat stopped moving. The horrible sick feeling of panic that blistered his nerves and made his stomach churn was just as bad as the awful void and the hard pavement so far below them.

Then he heard himself screaming. "Don't move this thing! Don't turn the wheel! We'll fall off if you do!"

His voice sounded ugly, hoarse and high-pitched with terror.

He wondered if anybody had heard him above the music and all the other noises below. But the wheel didn't move. They could probably be seen clearly from the ground. What was happening below? Was rescue on the way?

Very slowly and carefully he tried to move his head again to look down. The crowd below the wheel was growing fast; tiny, foreshortened figures were running from all over the park to join the sea of faces staring up at them. Directly below he could see Mrs. Jaleela in the grip of one of the men, hysterically waving her arms at them, crying and screaming. The other man had let go of Francine. She and Cookie had moved closer; they were both staring silently up at them. *Francine, Francine! Don't let them turn the wheel! We'll fall off. Tell them to get help. We're still alive, we're still okay. Tell them to rescue us!*

He opened his mind to listen, trying hard to hear Francine's faint thoughts through Noah's panic and Cookie's inarticulate agony. . . . *Idea . . . know what to do. . . . hear me? . . . got to try it . . . the only way. . . .*

If only their communication didn't diminish with distance that way! But all along it had been improving. If they just kept in contact, maybe it would get better now. *I can't hear you, I can't hear you! Louder, louder, as loud as you can!*

. . . calm, keep calm. . . . good idea. . . . Listen to

*me, try to listen. Noah . . . do it. . . . tell him what
to . . . make the thing . . .*

Her thoughts did seem stronger, but Noah's and
Cookie's powerful emotions still covered her up too
much. And both his arms were hurting badly now.
Hard metal bit painfully into his left arm; his right arm,
holding Noah, ached and quivered and felt weaker
every second. He didn't know how much longer he
could keep holding on. *Noah, Noah, be quiet! Stop
thinking at me! We've got to listen to Francine; she's
trying to tell us what to do. Shut up, Noah!*

Noah gasped, his head against Paul's neck, and his
small body shook. But his thoughts did waver and grow
quiet; and Francine, who seemed to be sending out her
message over and over again without stopping, came
through a little more clearly. *. . . fix seat . . . hold
it . . . place so . . . bring you . . . the ground. You
can tell me . . . secure, and I'll tell the man . . . to do.
Can you . . . me? Can you hear me?*

Again, Francine, tell me again!

*Noah . . . fix the seat. His power . . . psychokine-
sis . . . put the seat back . . . hold it there. He can
do . . . if he understands. Hold it in place . . . turn
the wheel . . . you back down.*

He squeezed Noah just a bit tighter. The seat wob-
bled again, the panic rose up again, but Paul froze and
in a moment the seat was steady once more. *Did you
hear that, Noah? Did you hear Francine?*

*I don't know what she means. I'm so scared I don't
know what she means.* But it was clear that Noah too
was trying to be brave, for there was less panic now.

116

Noah. Listen hard. You're a good boy and a brave boy. And you're special. You can do things nobody else in the world can do. You can think about things and make them move, like the flowers you gave us, and your teddy bear, and the man's newspaper on the subway. Is it easy for you to do that?

I never think about it; it just kind of happens when I want it to. You mean nobody else can do that?

No, you're the only one. The wind was gathering force and now Paul felt the whole wheel sigh and sway. The seat rocked terrifyingly. Only by making his whole body rigid and gripping the beam with every ounce of strength could Paul make the seat stop moving—and his strength was waning fast. *Noah, could you do that to this seat? Could you make this seat flat again, so it will hold us up? If you do that, Noah, they can bring us down to the ground again and we'll be okay. It's the only way. If you don't do it, we'll . . . we'll probably die, Noah. I can't keep holding on much longer.*

I . . . I never did anything that big before. Why can't somebody come up and get us?

The wind grew stronger, whining around the metal beams and the lights. The screams and babbling voices and music far below grew fainter and farther away as the wind sighed more persistently around them, cutting Paul and Noah off. Every time the wheel swayed, Paul felt his arm, burning with pain now, slip a little more, losing its grip on the beam. Perhaps they would eventually come with ladders or with nets to catch them, but that would be too late.

Paul was not strong, and now he was losing control.

His arm seemed to be detached from the rest of him; he wondered if it would hold for another minute. *There's no time for them to get here, Noah. I'm going to fall soon. Try it, Noah. Lift up the seat, make it flat like it was before, hold it there steady. As soon as they see that, they'll bring the wheel down. Noah, we're going to fall.*

He felt his arm begin to slip. He tried to hold it steady but it didn't seem to work; he felt no connection to it at all. *Noah! Noah! I'm fall—*

Then the seat lurched underneath him, ripping his throbbing arm away from the beam and rising up into the air. Rising up fast. Noah rolled away from him and slid back onto the seat. The loose end kept rising up in little jerks. Now it was higher than the attached end. It kept rising. He felt himself sliding toward Noah, who was crouched against the other armrest in a little ball, his eyes closed, concentrating. *Noah! Stop it! Look at what you're doing! Just hold it in place! It's going too high! Noah!*

But he could not reach Noah. This was probably the most difficult thing Noah had ever done, and he needed to concentrate, to focus all his power on it. *Flat, Noah! Keep it flat or we'll just fall off the other end!* Paul screamed at him with all the power he had.

Though Noah didn't open his eyes or respond, he must have heard Paul, because he then proceeded to make the seat level. But not by lowering the free end. Instead, he began raising up the attached end. *No, Noah! That won't work! Noah, you're going to—*

There was a terrible tearing sound as the wooden seat tried to pull itself away from the metal bar holding it to the wheel. The bar tried to drag it back, but Noah was raising the seat up, up, higher and higher, until with a screaming, grinding crunch the wood broke loose from the metal, leaving a gaping, splintery wound in the back of the seat where the bar had been attached. Level now, and free, the seat kept on rising.

Paul glanced down at the other people on the Ferris wheel. Before, they had been whimpering and comforting each other and wondering what to do and how they were ever going to get down. Now they forgot all that and simply gaped up at the floating Ferris wheel seat in utter bewilderment and disbelief.

Paul looked down. He realized that he was picking up a great wordless cry from the people on the ground far below. He and Noah were now about twenty feet higher than the Ferris wheel. He could just barely make out the tiny figures of Cookie, Mrs. Jaleela, Francine, and one of the men. The other man had disappeared.

Then he heard a siren, and looked toward the edge of the crowd. There were the flashing blue beacons of police cars, a white rescue van, and behind that the ungainly shape of a fire truck. There wasn't much the fire truck could do now, but, Paul assured himself, the rescue van might still come in handy.

Of course Paul was terrified. Who knew what Noah was going to do next? Still, this situation was an improvement over being trapped and panic-stricken, with his arm breaking and not knowing what to do and being sure they were going to die. If Noah could do this, he could certainly get them safely to the ground—if Paul could get him to do it.

He turned and looked at the small child beside him. Noah was still crouched into a ball with his eyes closed. The seat was vibrating rapidly, tickling Paul's rear end and making a strange whining hum. There almost seemed to be a kind of pale glow around Noah, encircling him and Paul and the Ferris wheel seat, which was still rising.

Noah! Paul tried again. *Noah! Look where we are, look what you're doing! Noah, you're taking us too high. Listen to me, Noah!*

Suddenly Noah opened his eyes and looked around them. In that second the seat dropped. *Noah!* Paul screamed as they plummeted down toward the Ferris wheel again. *Catch it, Noah! Catch it!*

Noah caught it, slapping them both sharply on the rear end as the seat swooped upwards and the crowd gasped again. But now Noah seemed to have gotten the hang of it. He clutched the bar in front of him, looking around excitedly as their ascent slowed and the seat finally came to rest, floating calmly in midair forty feet above the Ferris wheel and more than a hundred feet above the ground.

I can do it! I can do it! Noah cried out, blasting Paul with great billowing red clouds that flickered and sizzled with yellow bolts of lightning. *We don't even need that old Ferris wheel; I can do it myself!*

Noah, you're wonderful, you're fantastic! cried out Paul. *We can have so much fun, we can do this again and again. But right now, you better take us slowly slowly slowly down to the ground. Your mother's going crazy, she's so worried and afraid. Take us down slow so you can tell her you're okay.*

Oh, yes, she's never been this bad before, Noah agreed, and Paul marveled at his ability to hear her thoughts from this great a distance. *We better go back quick.*

Slow, Noah, take it slow, Paul cautioned him, as they began their descent. And Noah did manage to descend slowly, if not quite directly. When they reached the level of the Ferris wheel, the seat veered off to the side and circled around it. Noah waved and grinned at the people still gaping and shivering in their seats. *Why not?* thought Paul, and he waved and smiled at them himself.

Then he cupped his hands over his mouth and called out, "They'll bring you down now. As soon as we get back, we'll tell them to take you down. You're all going to be okay."

And Paul realized, as they glided gracefully closer to the earth, that the tremendous joy inside him was not coming just from his own relief at being saved. Nor was it coming from Noah and Cookie and Francine. It was that great cry from the whole crowd of people waiting below. Now he could hear their thoughts too, and that meant his own power was continuing to grow.

They were only about twenty feet from the ground.

He could see the tears streaming down Mrs. Jaleela's cheeks. The two men were together again, whispering to each other. Cookie was trotting in an excited circle and wagging her tail and barking up at them. Francine was smiling and crying at the same time. *Oh, Paul,* he heard her clearly now, *oh, I'm so glad I'm so glad, it was so terrible, but now everything's wonderful and we've won now and everything, but I'm the most glad about you, Paul.*

At the fifteen-foot level, Noah made one last little swoop, dipping down and almost touching the two men, who ducked and covered their heads with their hands. Then the seat rose up again, hovered for a moment before the crowd, and finally settled gently down to earth in the center of the empty space in front of the Ferris wheel.

10

In an instant Mrs. Jaleela had Noah in her arms, hugging him against her and rocking back and forth and sobbing. Cookie was hopping and barking around them. Then Francine had her arms around Paul and he was pressing his face against her hair. *Oh, I'm so glad I'm so glad it was so terrible I couldn't stand it I would have missed you so much it would have been so terrible about Noah but you if something had happened to you I don't know what I would do.*

It was you who saved us. I was too scared to think up there, I never would have thought of getting Noah to do that. It was you who saved us.

Paul felt a tap on his shoulder and they stepped

apart. It was a man in a white uniform, holding some kind of breathing apparatus, and behind him two more men with a stretcher.

"Are you all right?" the man said breathlessly. "Did you get hurt? How do you feel?"

"I . . . I guess I feel okay," Paul said, and shook his left arm. "My arm's a little sore, that's all. I'm okay."

"What about the little kid?" asked the man, still panting. He seemed to need the breathing apparatus more than Paul did.

"I'm sure he's fine," said Paul, "but you could go check."

He hurried over to Mrs. Jaleela. There were policemen on all sides, holding back the large, excited crowd around the Ferris wheel, and three more policemen talking to the two men who had been following them. The only other person who had gotten through the line of police into the clear space at the base of the wheel was an attractive, vaguely familiar young man, who approached Paul now, smiling. "Excuse me," he said, "but are you all right? You're not hurt or anything?"

"No," said Paul.

"Do you feel like talking? We've got to find out what happened up there!"

"Who are you?" Paul said suspiciously.

"Oh, he's okay," said Francine, wiping her eyes with the back of her hand and making dark smudges across her face.

"Tony Andrews, from channel 8 news," he said, and turned and pointed behind him. Beside the police cars,

Paul now noticed, was a large blue van, and next to it stood a man with a strange contraption on his shoulder. "And we have just taken the pictures of the century with our instant-eye camera."

"You mean . . . you mean you have movies of what happened up there?" Paul asked him.

"Videotapes. They've already been broadcast locally. And in a matter of hours, people will be watching them all over the world. Our pictures! But we have to know what happened up there. You were up there. What was it like? Are you all right? Do you know what happened?"

"Yes, I do know," said Paul.

"And we'll tell you everything," said Francine. "But first I want you to meet some people." She led him over to Noah and Mrs. Jaleela. The man in white hovered nearby, but did not seem to feel that Noah needed immediate attention. Mrs. Jaleela was still hugging Noah and crying, but she looked around when Francine and Paul and the newsman approached.

"This is Mrs. Jaleela, and her son Noah," explained Francine, "and Cookie, their dog. Noah happens to be the most amazing person on the face of the earth, and Cookie is the most amazing dog."

"Everything that happened up there, Noah did," said Paul.

"*Him?*" the newsman said, amazed.

"Him," insisted Francine. "Mrs. Jaleela," she said more gently, "oh, I'm sorry, I'm so sorry it had to be like this. But now do you believe us?"

"Oh, I don't know what to believe," Mrs. Jaleela said huskily. She ran her hand through Noah's hair. "Did you really do that, darling? Is it really true?"

Noah smiled at her, and nodded yes.

Mrs. Jaleela's eyes widened, and she held Noah out away from her. "Noah! Did you hear me? Can you hear?"

"Oh, he can hear what people say, I'm sure he can," said Francine. "When he bothers to listen, that is. Most of the time he hears a lot more than just what people say, so he doesn't pay that much attention to their voices and words."

"You're still not making this any clearer," the newsman said, shaking his head.

Mrs. Jaleela was hugging Noah again.

"Well, first I want you to meet some other people," said Francine, and she led him over to the two men and the policemen, who stepped back slightly as they approached. "Hello," Francine said pleasantly to the two men. "I don't know your names, but I'd like you to meet this newsman here, from channel 8. He'd like to know what's been going on here. Maybe you could explain your part in it."

The policemen, the newsman, Francine and Paul looked at them expectantly. In that moment, any doubts Paul ever might have had about the motives of the two men fell away. Their thoughts were far vaguer to him than Francine's, but he could just begin to make them out. They were not pleasant. There was no joy and relief, no enthusiasm about Paul's and Noah's miraculous escape. Instead, there was only a kind of angry disappointment that included a lot of hostility toward him and even more toward Francine.

And, though they had clearly heard Francine's request, they refused to speak.

"Well, if you won't talk to him, then I'd like to ask you a question myself," said Francine. "Something I've been wondering about. How did you find out about Noah, anyway?"

The two men looked at each other. Then one of them said, "We've had some other reports about that same UFO. We followed one of them up, and it seemed interesting enough to make it worthwhile to—"

"We don't have anything to say," the other man interrupted, glancing blandly but significantly at the one who had been talking. "It's time for us to get back." He turned to the newsman. "How wide an area do those instant-eye broadcasts cover?" he asked him.

"The whole state, at least," said the newsman quickly. "But they also get us in—"

The man didn't wait for him to finish. "Come on," he said to the other one, and started walking away. The other man looked at Francine briefly, then turned and joined his friend. In a moment they were lost in the crowd.

The newsman looked after them, shaking his head. "Crazy," he said. "We had to fight that one guy off in order to get our pictures. Good thing the other one wasn't around then; they might have really stopped us."

"Where was he?" Paul asked Francine.

"He must have gone to call *headquarters,* or something, to ask them what to do next," she said.

"Yeah, and it's a good thing you were there too, honey," said the newsman. He turned to the policemen. "This little kid really can fight," he said. "She kept that guy away from the camera more than *I* did!"

"But what was it all about?" asked one of the policemen.

"Well, they wanted to keep Noah secret," said Francine. "But now that everybody knows about him there isn't anything else they can do."

"But who are they?" said the newsman. "Everything happened so fast I never had a chance to find out."

"Oh, they're from some kind of government agency," Francine told him. "They've been following Noah and us around for a while. For pretty obvious reasons, they wanted to use him for their own purposes. They were going to take him away and keep him secret so they could channel his power instead of letting him develop it naturally."

"But why were they following you?"

"Because we have mental telepathy too," said Paul. "But not as much as Noah. So they wanted to use us, but they were also afraid we would get in the way of what they wanted to do to Noah. And they were right. But I still don't understand how they found out so much about—"

Suddenly Francine grabbed him by the shoulder. "Paul!" she cried out. "Don't you remember? We . . . they were on the elevator with us, in the library. And

129

before that, the drugstore. It *was* them; now I remember! They probably already knew a little bit, and then we gave the rest away. How *could* we?"

The newsman was still shaking his head as he took out a pen and a pad of paper. "I'd think you two kids were crazy if I hadn't seen that . . . that thing with my own eyes," he said. "But now you'd better tell me everything. Keep calm. Just start at the beginning." He beckoned to another man who was still standing by the van. "Come on over here, Harry!" he called out. "Bring the tape recorder. We'll get some more visuals after they tell us their story."

"Mrs. Jaleela has to hear it too," said Francine.

Mrs. Jaleela, still holding Noah, was a bit calmer now. She listened, along with the two newsmen and the policemen, as Paul and Francine told their story. They started at the beginning, with the dream, interrupting each other frequently, and finished with the amazing events at the Ferris wheel.

"I never thought it would end so . . . so perfectly," said Francine. "There were some pretty horrible moments there."

"Well, you kids certainly have a lot of guts," said the newsman.

"It wasn't us as much as Cookie," said Francine. "Cookie did everything, really. If it wasn't for her, they'd have us and Noah now, and nobody would know anything about it, and . . . and who knows what they would be able to do with us!"

"It's all just so . . . so difficult to believe," Mrs.

Jaleela said softly. She kissed Noah gently on the forehead. "I still . . . I still don't really know what to think."

"I can understand your problem," said one of the policemen. "But lady, what we all just saw was pretty convincing."

"And for so long I thought I was going mad," Mrs. Jaleela said, and sighed. "What a relief to know I'm not."

"But what did those two men say to you?" Francine asked her. "How did they get you on their side?"

"Well, they really didn't explain very much." Mrs. Jaleela adjusted Noah in her arms. He was now resting his head sleepily on her shoulder, not emitting much of anything except vague wisps of calmness and contentment. "They said they had found out that Noah was a very exceptional child, much more important than I realized. And then they asked to see him and I didn't know what to say; I was confused. Then they asked me if you two children were there, and they started telling me that you were interfering with important plans and that you would be dangerous for Noah. And then, of course, I was even more frightened, and we went into his room, and he was gone. Oh, it was terrible!" Her eyes dimmed with tears again, and she stroked Noah's hair.

"You two kids sure got in way over your heads," said one of the policemen. "I tell you, you're lucky it turned out the way it did. I don't think I would have done the same thing if I'd been in your shoes."

"But don't you think we were right?" demanded Francine, looking around at the group. "If they just wanted to do what was good for Noah, why would they think we were dangerous?"

"Oh, I don't doubt that you're right about them," the newsman said. "You just took a pretty big risk, that's all. You could very easily have made everything a lot worse." Francine angrily tried to interrupt him, but the newsman ignored her and went on. "But if you wanted to get everything out into the open and convince the world about Noah, you definitely succeeded, that is for sure." He was sounding more and more excited now. "This story is going to change the world, no doubt about it. It's going to change your lives and it is also, incidentally, going to change mine—and to tell you the truth I cannot *wait* to break the whole thing! And all we were expecting was a routine story on this park. Man! Come on, let's get some pictures of all of you, over by the Ferris wheel seat."

They posed, smiling stiffly, while the camera whirred, Noah and Mrs. Jaleela in the middle, with Paul and Francine on either side, and Cookie in front. They were getting impulses of minor discomfort from Cookie, brought on by the unfamiliar men and the camera and all the attention. But underneath that, her mind was more at ease than it had ever been in all the time they had known her.

The police suggested that they ride home in the rescue van, with a police escort for protection, and the newsman insisted on going with them. Paul and Fran-

cine walked over to the van behind the others, with Cookie. She had not had a chance to thank them yet, and kept stopping to lick their hands and faces, emitting waves of gratitude and joy and relief and undying friendship. But also, just before they entered the van, she did flash them briefly with a sharp impulse of admonishment, and the image of the lights from the dream.

I wish she wouldn't do that, Paul complained. *It does make me feel guilty.*

They climbed into the backseat with Cookie. Mrs. Jaleela, holding Noah, sat in the front with the driver and the newsman. The two other medical men sat in the area behind the backseat, which was filled with all kinds of complicated medical equipment.

Well, Francine answered him, *She's just annoyed that we didn't pay more attention to what she was trying to tell us. It all worked out great, but she thinks it would have been safer if we hadn't come to Wonderland at all.*

There were more policemen now, parting the crowd in front of the police car and the van as they crunched over the gravel toward the exit from the park. The colored lights had been turned off, the buildings were gray shapes in the darkness, and the crowd around the Ferris wheel was slowly dispersing. *But that's something I was wondering about,* thought Paul as the van drove out through the gateway. *How did she know? Those lights in the dream were the same as the lights on the Ferris wheel! She knew something like the seat breaking was going to happen, and she was trying to prevent it, to keep us away. Do you understand me, Francine?*

You don't mean that Cookie can predict—

The future! interrupted Paul. He looked down at Cookie, curled up between them, asleep already, her head in Francine's lap. *Yes, in some way she must be able to. Of course, she was getting bad vibrations from the two men, and she was trying to get us to save Noah from them. And she was telling us who Noah was and everything, and that was the main part of the dream. But she also had some idea how it was going to turn out, not very clear, not the whole thing, just a kind of warning about the future.*

Do you think Noah has that too? she asked him.

He must. But probably it just hasn't developed yet. Remember, Cookie has a grown-up dog's brain, and Noah's is still hardly developed at all.

And look what he can do already! Wow, what's he going to be like when he grows up?

"You're sure you're not going to mention our names or where we live or anything like that?" Mrs. Jaleela was asking the newsman.

"No, not on the next broadcast anyway," he assured her. "And you know the police will be protecting you. But I expect that from now on you'll be dealing with scientists and doctors instead of secret agents. Noah is going to be one studied and tested little boy, I promise you."

"I suppose there's no way we can prevent that," murmured Mrs. Jaleela. Noah was sleeping now, and she looked down at him, her face beginning to tighten with worry once again.

"No way," said the newsman. "But he will be protected, now that it's all out in the open. They'll try to keep it quiet, try to keep him pretty much out of the public eye, I'm sure, once the first blast of publicity dies down. The people you'll be dealing with now will be concerned with his welfare, you see, just as much as you are. He's a national resource, it's true, but now it's too late for anyone to use him as a secret weapon, and that's all to the good."

Noah, with his head on his mother's shoulder, dreamily opened his eyes and smiled at Paul and Francine. *So nice now . . . Cookie not worried any more. She's been worrying for so long, but now it's over. And now I have you too, Paul and Francine. So nice . . . the way you can understand me . . . so nice . . .* and his eyelids began drifting down again.

Only to snap open, suddenly, the same instant that Paul and Francine stiffened in the backseat. Though the black and white images that rushed into their heads were vague and dreamlike, the emotions of fear and warning they contained were not vague at all.

Cookie whined deep in her throat and scratched at the air with her paw. She twisted her head in Francine's lap and then with a little whimper began to relax again as the images faded and grew dim.

But before they had a chance to react, the newsman looked back over his shoulder at Paul and Francine.

"You two are being pretty quiet back there," he said jovially. "I'll bet you're wondering what it's going to feel like to be celebrities, huh?"

Paul looked down at Cookie again, and shivered. He was not wondering what it would feel like to be a celebrity. He was wondering what he was going to dream that night.

WILLIAM SLEATOR is the author of many outstanding science fiction novels for young readers, including *Interstellar Pig*, an ALA Notable Book; *Among the Dolls*; and most recently, *Strange Attractors*. A composer as well as a writer, Mr. Sleator lives in Boston.

RUTH SANDERSON, attended the Paier School of Art in Hamden, Connecticut, and has been illustrating children's books since her graduation in 1974. She has always been a fan of science fiction, so she found illustrating this book especially enjoyable. Ms. Sanderson lives in Bethany, Connecticut.